Free Legal Adv...
Please be advised tha...
or not returning bo...
other library materials is a
crime punishable by law

MOSTLY GHOSTS

WITHDRAWN

Terror
Under
the
Tent

OTHER YEARLING BOOKS YOU WILL ENJOY:

YEARLING BOOKS/YOUNG YEARLINGS/YEARLING CLASSICS are designed especially to entertain and enlighten young people. Charles F. Reasoner, Professor Emeritus of Children's Literature and Reading, New York University, is consultant to this series.

For a complete listing of all Yearling titles, write to
Dell Readers Service, P.O. Box 1045,
South Holland, IL 60473.

PB
J
AND

MOSTLY GHOSTS

Terror Under the Tent

by Mary Anderson

CHESTER PUBLIC LIBRARY
CHESTER, ILLINOIS

A YEARLING BOOK

Published by
Dell Publishing Co., Inc.
1 Dag Hammarskjold Plaza
New York, New York 10017

Copyright © 1987 by Mary Anderson

All rights reserved. No part of this book may be reproduced or transmitted in any form or by any means, electronic or mechanical, including photocopying, recording or by any information storage and retrieval system, without the written permission of the Publisher, except where permitted by law.

Yearling ® TM 913705, Dell Publishing Co., Inc.

ISBN: 0-440-48633-5

Printed in the United States of America

November 1987

10 9 8 7 6 5 4 3

CW

MOSTLY GHOSTS

Terror
Under
the
Tent

CHESTER PUBLIC LIBRARY
CHESTER, ILLINOIS

Chapter One

MRS. BARCLAY, THE HISTORY TEACHER, STARED OUT THE classroom window to admire the magnolia trees. "The people that once bestowed commands," she quoted, "now long eagerly for just two things—bread and circuses." She turned toward the class. "I'm paraphrasing, of course, but that statement is as true today as when it was written two thousand years ago by the Roman poet Juvenal."

"Juvenile is right," Jamie whispered. "Old Barclay has spring fever again."

His sister, Amy, agreed. "Last year she danced barefoot in the Cartwright Memorial Fountain. What do you suppose she'll do this year?"

"To quote a more contemporary source," Mrs. Barclay went on, " 'the first day of spring is one thing, and the first spring day is another' . . . therefore, I'm obliged to give you a history assignment over your spring recess."

The entire class groaned.

"A pleasant one," she assured them. "Since the circus will be coming to town tomorrow, I'd like you to research its history. Circuses are even older than the poet Juvenal."

"I liked old Barclay better when she was barefoot and bananas!" said Amy disgustedly.

Hearing the dismissal bell ring, the class quickly shoved their history books into the desk and stampeded toward the door.

Amy was the first one in the hallway. She'd been looking forward to spring recess for ages: two whole weeks to do whatever she wanted—which meant doing absolutely nothing! She slowly strolled past the garden of Hillcrest, only half aware of her surroundings. She barely heard the riotous noise of the younger students screeching the proverbial "no more pencils, no more books" as they pushed against her. She wasn't even aware that her brother was walking along behind her.

"Hey, stupid, are you blind or what?" Jamie shouted.

Amy's reverie was quickly broken.

"You nearly walked into that tree. Do you need glasses?"

"No, I need to be left alone."

Jamie shoved a stack of books into his schoolbag. "Excuse me! Sounds like a major case of spring fever. Be careful or *you'll* be wading in the Cartwright Fountain too. Even though old Barclay's strange, she gave us a great assignment. I can't wait to start."

Amy was always amazed at how different twins can be. In their twelve years, she and Jamie had rarely shared an opinion about anything. "You *want* to do that dumb report?"

"Sure. Dad once mentioned the Circus Maximus, but I'd no idea it went back to ancient Roman days. Just think, Julius Caesar was a circus fan."

"Fascinating," said Amy, totally unfascinated.

"You think they had popcorn back in those days?"

Amy didn't care. As they walked along, she noticed a field of flowers in full bloom. "Look, Jamie, daffodils. Aren't they beautiful?"

"Yeah, great," he said, barely noticing. "Let's get over to the library before all the good circus books are gone. I saw Nelson Rappaport race over there. He'd better not get a higher grade than me on this report."

"Don't worry, you'll get an A plus."

"Really?" he asked. "How do you know? Did you have another psychic vision?"

"Why should I waste my psychic powers on that? You *always* get an A plus."

"Well, it doesn't hurt to be sure."

"What'd happen if you got a B once in your life, Jamie?"

"I'd know I wasn't working hard enough. What'd happen if *you* got a B?"

Amy sighed. "I'd know I'd died and gone to heaven! Let's not talk about schoolwork. Spring vacation just started."

Jamie disagreed. "My vacation won't start until I've written this report. You'd better get busy on yours too. But don't count on me for help—it's every twin for himself."

"I don't need your help," Amy snapped.

Jamie knew exactly what she was thinking. "Dad won't help you either; not when he finds out this is a school report. You'd better come to the library with me."

9

Amy refused. The thought of being imprisoned in a stale old building filled with dusty books was dreadful.

"C'mon," he coaxed, "all the best reference books will be gone by tomorrow."

Amy didn't care if the best books disappeared from the Monroe library forever. "I'm taking a walk through the woods."

"It's your funeral," he warned her. He ran ahead in the direction of the library, hoping Nelson Rappaport hadn't already grabbed all the goodies from the shelves.

Amy walked toward Miller's Pond. She knew of a crocus patch there just beyond the elm trees, and she was eager to see if it was blooming.

Chapter Two

AMY HAD A GLORIOUS WALK, DURING WHICH SHE OBSERVED every fledgling flower coming into bloom. She arrived home dreamy-eyed, barely noticing her parents seated in the living room.

"Did you go for a walk?" asked her mother.

"Yes, Mom."

"Where to?" asked her father.

Amy sighed, slowly climbing the stairs. "Nowhere."

Miriam Ferguson had only glimpsed her daughter but knew the symptoms of spring fever. "I don't think Amy will be down for dinner, Richard."

Mr. Ferguson nodded and smiled in agreement.

Sitting on her window seat, Amy stared into the backyard. The apple trees weren't in bloom yet, but tiny bursts of buds promised they soon would be. Amy was intrigued that something so old could become new again

11

CHESTER PUBLIC LIBRARY
CHESTER, ILLINOIS

each spring. Her ancestor, Lieutenant Colonel Jebediah Aloysious Tredwell, had planted the trees more than two hundred years earlier. They were now all that remained of his beloved apple orchard.

As Amy stared at their branches, she realized she hadn't thought of Jebediah in quite a while—not since the last time his spirit had appeared to her. What did the apple trees look like in his day? she wondered. Did the blossoms smell as sweet? She would've liked to ask Jeb about that.

Deep in reverie, Amy heard a soft voice from behind her, as if someone were whispering into her ear. The voice was familiar. "As saplings," the voice explained, "they survived many a cruel winter because their roots were strong. Thus they have endured the vicissitudes of time."

Amy quickly glanced around. The spirit of her ancestor, Jebediah, had begun to materialize.

Amy never ceased to be amazed that her psychic ability enabled her to conjure up the spirit of Jebediah, the Revolutionary War hero, and she never failed to be impressed by his appearance. Wearing his powdered wig, embroidered waistcoat, shining black boots, and military uniform, his form was always impeccable.

"Jeb," she said with surprise, "you must've been reading my mind."

The lieutenant colonel stared out the window. "Perhaps. Or perhaps our minds are one regarding my apple trees. Many a spring I spent tending them, whereby I learned that if the seed be good and the root be strong, they will most likely tend themselves. As in all things,

God and Nature shall provide. But at this time of year I feel the desire to tend them myself once again. Does that not sound curious?"

"It sounds like spring fever," Amy said. "I've got it too." A disturbing thought crossed her mind. "There's nothing wrong, is there, Jeb? I mean, usually I see you only when something terrible is about to happen!"

Jebediah smiled. "How could anything dreadful occur on such a day as this, Cousin?"

Amy agreed but she was still confused. In the past Jebediah had appeared only to warn her of some danger. So what was he doing here *now?* "Don't get me wrong, I'm glad to see you. But *I* didn't summon you, did I?"

"I was undoubtedly in your thoughts," explained the spirit.

"Does that mean my psychic powers are getting stronger, Jeb?"

"Or mine perhaps; I cannot say. But what does it matter? On such a day as this all things are possible."

Amy agreed. "I'm sorry your beautiful apple orchard is gone, Jeb. There are only a few trees left."

"All things must change," he said, "yet nothing truly dies." Jebediah pointed toward the yard where a robin was building a nest in the bough of an apple tree. "Look you, Cousin, another harbinger of the season's bounty."

"Signs of spring are everywhere," said Amy. "The circus is coming to town tomorrow."

"The circus?" Jeb said enthusiastically. "What more concrete evidence of the season could one ask for? It would be ingratitude not to rejoice and insensibility not to participate."

13

"Right," said Amy. "Jamie and I can hardly wait."

"How fare things with your brother, Cousin?"

"Oh, he's okay. Annoying, as usual. Right now he's at the library working on some dumb report."

Jeb didn't pay much attention to Amy's response, for his mind was clearly elsewhere. "Ah, the circus." He sighed. "Nothing can stir the blood like its daring feats of horsemanship and acrobatics, its high-wire walkers and contortionists."

"Have you been to the circus?" she asked.

"What man or boy has not? There is nothing on this earth to rival it, as nothing ever shall. As in many things, General Washington and I were in agreement on that."

"You mean you went to the circus with General Washington?"

"Indeed. Many times. George was president by then, so the honor was all the greater. You see, Washington's presence guaranteed the respectability of such an entertainment. Ah, yes," Jeb mused, "it was April 1793. John Ricketts, a famous equestrian, had recently established the first circus company in the United States and had built amphitheaters in New York City and Philadelphia. Hitherto one had to travel to the Continent for such amusement, until Ricketts brought the magic of the circus to our own shores."

"Really?" Amy said. "Does that mean this guy Ricketts invented the American circus?"

"Not exactly, Cousin. Invention of the circus as we know it must go to Philip Astley. I'm proud to say he was a fellow military man, albeit an *Englishman*. A clever fellow, nonetheless. Astley discovered that by galloping

14

on his steed while standing upright in a circle, he could use centrifugal force to keep his balance. And thus the first modern circus ring was formed."

"Sounds like you know a lot about circus history, Jeb."

Jebediah nodded. "Much of it personally observed from a ringside seat," he said proudly. The spirit began to walk around the room as he expanded on the topic that had evoked so many colorful memories. He raised his hands with a flourish, as if reliving the experience. "Picture this, Cousin. Midst an unbroken ring of spectators, emotions would create a charged current and then the spectacle would begin. From within the audience, beggar, carpenter, poet, and princess alike, all would gasp at the wondrous feats performed."

As Amy listened to her ghostly ancestor, an idea came to her—an extremely clever idea. Jeb seemed to be a walking history of the circus, so why should she bother to read boring books? *Jeb* could be her reference material! Amy quickly ran to her desk and took our a notepad and pencil. "Tell me everything you know, Jeb: I'm fascinated."

"All of mankind is fascinated by the circus," he replied. "Maxentius, Domitian, Hadrian, and Nero built their Colosseums to enhance the spectacle. Centuries earlier the Egyptians had mile-long circus parades to honor their god Serapis."

Amy began writing feverishly.

"Ah, the sawdust," Jebediah sighed, then continued: "The smell of tanbark, the pungent animal odors—the very thought brings back my gnawing circus hunger. If I could only see it all but once again!"

"Facts, Jeb; just the facts," said Amy. "Do you know

15

the names of any other Roman emperors who had circus fever?"

"Augustus, naturally. Although the Circus Maximus had odious aspects, for thousands of beasts were killed. In those days encounters between man and beast always ended fatally."

"That's awful."

"Indeed so. Happily, no such violence mars the present spectacle. Now only pleasure and grandeur remain."

"What about snake charmers and magicians?" asked Amy. "Did they have those in your day too?"

Jebediah bristled at the question. "Conjurers? Indubitably. Such legerdemain is older than the pyramids. And charlatans as well," he added angrily. "Those who taint the magic of illusion with their false occultism."

"Don't you like magicians, Jeb?"

"I heartily approve the innocence of magical illusion," he explained, "but there have been those who have used this human fascination to ill advantage. Mark me, Cousin, be ever watchful for such men."

Jebediah's mood had suddenly changed, and then it dawned on Amy that he hadn't materialized merely to observe the budding of his apple trees. As always, Jeb had come to deliver a prophetic warning. She felt a faint psychic twinge, which quickly passed, so Amy thought nothing more of it. "You mean *evil* magicians?" she asked. "Did you ever meet one?"

"The most infamous one of all, dear Cousin. My travels on the Continent put me in contact with various villains, but Cagliostro was among the most villainous."

"Cagliostro? I think I may have heard that name before."

"History has marked him in infamy, as well it should," said Jebediah. "Despite his proclaimed magical powers, I found him to be a fool, rattle-pate, windbag, and swindler. And evil into the bargain."

"Really? You mean he was a phony?"

"Oh, he had powers, to be sure, but he used them only to enhance his personal adulation and wealth."

"What kinds of awful things did he do?" Amy asked. She was curious now.

Jeb seemed reluctant to elaborate. "We must speak no more of him. Suffice it to say that strong as the powers of good be in the universe, there are equally strong channels of evil. If a man be not moral, he may harness these elements. Those adept in the Ancient Knowledge yet lacking a moral sense can and will abuse the forces of the universe. This is the crudest, darkest use of such Divine Energy."

"You mean *black magic?*" Amy said.

The late afternoon sun had begun to fade into pinks and lavenders, and Jebediah himself seemed to be fading as well. "As always, my time here has been far too brief," he said. "Yet never forget the thread which binds us together, my child. Though it be invisible, it cannot be broken. Farewell for now."

Standing by the window, Jebediah's spirit slowly dissolved into smoky wisps, which drifted out to blend with the clouds on the horizon.

As Amy watched him depart she was left with a strangely uneasy, incomplete feeling.

But she was also left with a few pages of fascinating circus notes!

Chapter Three

JAMIE RETURNED HOME FURIOUS. NELSON RAPPAPORT HAD practically devoured every decent book in the Monroe Library. Nelson wasn't the star of the school track team for nothing!

"That guy raced through the shelves like lightning," Jamie complained. "By the time I arrived, he'd picked the place clean. There ought to be a law against *hoarding* books."

Mr. Ferguson was sympathetic. "What are you researching, Son?"

"The circus. Mrs. Barclay gave us a history project over the holiday."

"Amy didn't mention that," said Mrs. Ferguson.

"Amy's too busy sniffing flowers," Jamie grumbled as he stomped up the stairs. "Some people don't care about anything important!"

Jamie's parents stared at each other, the same thought running through both their minds. They hoped the twins' spring vacation wouldn't be filled with too many temperamental outbursts!

As Jamie walked past his sister's room he got a peculiar feeling. He pushed open her door. "Is everything okay in here?"

"Sure, why shouldn't it be? How'd it go at the library?"

"Rotten. Nelson the Vulture picked the shelves clean. I'll never get an A now." Throwing himself onto his sister's bed, Jamie noticed her notes lying there. "What's this?" he asked, scanning the pages. "Where did you get all this information? How'd you learn George Washington was a circus fan?"

"I have my ways," Amy said mysteriously. "All information isn't found in books, you know."

"You wouldn't know a book if it bit you, so how'd you learn this stuff?"

Amy grabbed the notepad from her brother's hand. "I don't have to tell you anything. Like you said, it's every twin for herself."

And then it hit him. "Jebediah has been here, hasn't he?" Jamie said. "*He* told you all this stuff. You couldn't get Dad to help you, so you got a ghost to do it instead!"

"What if I did? What's it to you?"

Jamie was furious. "Of all the dirty, sneaky, lazy . . ." He grabbed back the notepad. "You've got to share these facts with *me*, Amy."

"Who says so?" she argued, ripping the pad from her brother's hands and quickly shoving it into her drawer.

"*I* say so," he yelled. "If you don't share those facts, I'm telling Mom and Dad where you got them. They'd be mighty interested to learn you're psychic, and that you can conjure up our ancestor. It'd make fascinating dinner conversation, don't you think?"

Amy glared at her brother. He had sworn to keep her secret *forever*. The last thing in the world she wanted was to be considered weird because of her powers. "Jamie, you *promised*."

"I'd hate to break my promise, but if you're going to sneak around making Jeb do your work for you . . ."

"Oh, all right," she conceded. Amy took the notepad from her desk and threw it toward her brother. "Why's it so important you get A's all the time, anyway?"

"Thanks," he said smugly. "Let me know the next time Jeb appears so I can have a pencil ready."

"It wouldn't do you any good," she shouted. "You can't see or hear him, and you never will. You may be smart, Jamie, but you don't have any— Well, whatever it is you need to see spirits—you have none!"

"Don't worry, I'll get by," he said, slamming the door. He took the notes to his room, where he quickly copied them down.

When Jamie had finished, he lay down and stared out the window, waiting for dinnertime. He felt strangely uneasy. He hadn't liked blackmailing his sister into sharing her information; he had had to.

But something Amy had said bothered him. Getting A's *was* all-important to him. Being the best at whatever he did had always been imperative to Jamie, and lately it had become even more vital. Why? he wondered. He had

20

a good mind; no one argued that. He was worlds brighter than his sister, and yet that didn't seem to be enough.

As Jamie lay thinking, he finally admitted to himself something that he had always been reluctant to acknowledge: He was *jealous* of Amy. True, he had talents: cleverness, ambition, problem solving abilities his sister could never hope to equal. But Amy had something he would never have: instincts, intuition, and special sensitivities.

If only he, too, could see or hear Jebediah . . . only once be made aware of the Universal Force that caused the spirit to appear, if only . . . as Jamie closed his eyes he thought he felt a soft breeze blowing through the room. Then he thought he heard a faint voice, so muffled it was barely audible. "Be not so fretful, James," the voice said. "Deep within, all mankind is gifted with such powers; would you but know how to use them."

Of course, he thought he had only imagined hearing the voice, and it was quickly followed by a much more familiar one.

"Dinner's ready, kids," his mother shouted from the kitchen. "Come and get it."

Chapter Four

"WHAT'S THIS SWEET STUFF ON THE BAKED BEANS?" ASKED Jamie.

"Blackstrap molasses," said his mother. "When I was little, Grandma Tredwell always called it her spring tonic. Judging from your behavior this afternoon, I thought you *both* could use some."

"The only tonic these kids need is a visit to the circus," Mr. Ferguson said. "I can hardly wait for the Fanzini Troupe to arrive in town tomorrow. I saw their posters and they look like an impressive company."

"Now, Richard," his wife said jokingly. "You're not going to threaten to run away and join them, are you?"

"Why not? Waldo Simpson did."

"Who's he?" Amy asked.

"He was a physics professor at Monroe University until six years ago. Then he auditioned for the Ringling

22

Brothers' clown school and got accepted. Waldo threw away his books and now he travels all around the world—a very happy man, I might add."

"Maybe Mrs. Barclay could join up this year," Amy said hopefully. Her stupid assignment had already spoiled the beginning to Amy's holiday and caused a nasty fight with Jamie.

"Admit it, Miriam," Mr. Ferguson said, "wouldn't you like to run away and join the circus too?"

Mrs. Ferguson smiled at her husband. "I suppose, at times we all would. When I was little, I fantasized about becoming a bareback rider. I guess the circus has a kind of magic nothing else can compete with."

"Not even floppy disks or music videos," added Mr. Ferguson. "You're right, nothing can compete with live tigers and elephants! Kids, did I ever tell you I once fell in love with a snake enchantress?"

"Are you serious?" Jamie said.

"Son, when you're thirteen, you're *always* serious. Her act was called Seraphina and Her Serpents. Seraphina was the most gorgeous female I'd ever seen (until I met your mother, naturally). She had three trained pythons who crawled around her body like ants. I was so enamored, I devoured every book on snakes I could find. Then I sneaked into her circus trailer, hoping to impress her with my vast knowledge. I told Seraphina that in Greek mythology the python was said to have dwelt in the caves of Mount Parnassus until Apollo slew him. Know what Seraphina said? 'If anyone messes with *my* snakes, I hit him with a hard salami!' It seems Seraphina kept a salami in her trailer as a weapon to ward off possible intruders. That remark made me love her even more. That woman was my first superhero!"

Amy giggled. It was funny to think of her superstudious academic father in love with a snake charmer!

"I was in love with a superhero myself," said Mrs. Ferguson, not to be outdone. "When I was in high school, a circus troupe came to town starring Bruno the Lion Tamer. He could actually put his head into a lion's mouth."

"I hope the lion didn't have bad breath," joked Jamie. "That'd make a powerful stench."

"And your great-grandmother once fell in love with Houdini," she added, "while watching his water-torture act."

"Let's face it," Mr. Ferguson sighed—"circus performers are magical people. While we *dream* of adventure, they live it. Even the smell of the circus is magical."

"That's what Jeb said too," Amy added, before realizing what she had said.

"Who's Jeb?" her mother asked.

"Just one of Amy's friends," Jamie said teasingly. "*I've* never seen him. I think he only likes *weirdos*."

Amy banged her spoon onto her plate, causing molasses to spurt into Jamie's eye. "So sorry, Brother dear, but Mom says it's good for you."

The next morning many citizens of Monroe were standing on Main Street eagerly awaiting the arrival of the Fanzini Troupe and its parade through town. Several days earlier posters had appeared around town announcing the unique event: THE FANZINI CIRCUS, A TRUE OLD-FASHIONED SPECTACLE.

24

Older townspeople could fondly remember the many circuses that, during their youth, had passed through town each spring. But the true magical splendor of the circus parade was more or less a thing of the past—though not to the Fanzinis. This troupe had tried to maintain all the richness and charming traditions that had long been the hallmark of a traveling one-ring circus, including the now seldom-seen parade through town.

Rufus Shuttleworth, one of Monroe's oldest citizens, felt a surge of youthful exuberance when he heard the words he had been privileged to hear so many times as a boy: "Hold your horses—the elephants are coming!"

The first muted strains of a calliope sounded in the distance, and a wave of blood-tingling excitement passed through the waiting crowd.

"My word, a calliope." Ethel Rutherford (another of Monroe's most senior citizens) sighed as she spoke. "I haven't seen one since I was a girl!"

As the elaborately painted steam organ rolled down Main Street whistling a familiar circus melody, a procession of pachyderms followed. Six massive elephants shuffled along single file. All wore bejeweled blankets. A small pavilion sat on the back of the lead elephant, and the lovely passenger, who wore a brilliant sequined cape, waved toward the crowd. Next came the team of horses with costumed bareback riders whose plumes fluttered in the breeze. More horses followed. Bedecked in brass trimming and monogrammed harnesses, they pulled the cage wagons.

Squeals of delight rose from the children along the parade route as the wagon loads of wild animals passed by, and everyone gasped when Julio, the fearless lion tamer, rolled by, seated among his pride of roaring lions.

There were wood-carved floats and a delightful children's band mounted on Shetland ponies, and a man banging a copper kettledrum that gleamed in the morning sunlight.

Naturally, clowns added a comic element to the festivities, and their antics amused the curbstone audience.

The wooden wheels of the circus vehicles were painted yellow, orange, and red, and looked like rolling sunbursts as they moved down the avenue. The sides of the wagon were decorated with intricate carvings of monsters, goddesses, and gold-leaf scrolls.

Perhaps even more spectacular to Amy than all the ornateness of the circus paraphernalia was the splendor of the circus horses. She admired the majestic rosinback horses as they trotted along with sequined riders on their backs. They had great arched necks and deep soft eyes, and Amy knew they were called the aristocrats of the ring for their perfect conformation and gait.

Jamie was particularly impressed by Signore Armando Fanzini, circus manager and lead performer of the Flying Fanzinis wire act. Jamie had read all the posters beforehand and had noticed that mostly all the acts bore the name of Fanzini: acrobats, tumblers, high-wire walkers, riders. This man with his long brown handlebar mustache was the patriarch of a most amazing circus dynasty. No longer a young man, he marched through the streets with the pride and energy of someone half his age.

Madame Lorenza Fanzini was equally impressive. The ringmaster of the troupe, she followed behind her husband, cracking a whip in the air to announce the time of that evening's performance. She stood straight and stiff as a rod; her luxuriant black hair was braided into a bun. But behind all the grandeur of her appearance Jamie sensed a motherly warmth.

Jamie also noticed the circus flyers. They were all wearing beaded tights, capes, and leotards. Surprisingly, half of them were *boys*, who managed not to look silly in the outfits. Jamie glanced at one boy, probably his own age, seated atop a circus wagon and waving at the crowd. What was it like to be a member of a circus? he wondered. To travel throughout the country, maybe the world, with the sound of applause constantly ringing in your ears? Surely, it in no way resembled his own dull life in Monroe!

The magical parade seemed endless. The twins now observed a wagon with clowns bouncing about on a trampoline, and a charming cart filled with performing dogs dressed in coats and tutus. Then came a cluster of monkeys crawling around the sides of a giant barrel.

The most spectacular performer in the Fanzini Circus had been saved for the finale of the parade. He was the Great Loogastric, magician and illusionist *extraordinaire*. His act had been featured on all of the posters:

LOOGASTRIC, THE GRAND COPT, WITH POWERS
LEARNED FROM ANCIENT EGYPT

All the advertising hype hadn't prepared Jamie for the impressive figure who now walked slowly down Main Street. The crowd seemed to grow silent as he appeared.

The calliope music, the blare of the band, and the resounding kettledrum all ceased as the Great Loogastric rounded the corner. His arrival needed no further fanfare.

Loogastric was a small man, but his mere presence in the crowd was something to note. He did not wave to the onlookers as all the other performers had. Instead, he cupped his hands under a large crystal ball and stared into the distance. His long black silk robe was embroidered with red hieroglyphs. On his head he wore a gold turban ornamented with jewels, and around his neck were gold chains to which strange religious symbols were attached.

Amy stared at the magician. His face was surely one of the most remarkable she had ever seen. Not actually ugly, but certainly unattractive. Above all, his eyes fascinated her. They were almost indescribable. Of supernatural depths comprising both fire and ice, they were eyes that could enthrall the mind and paralyze the will . . . *evil* eyes.

Amy remembered, almost involuntarily, Jeb's offhanded comment regarding the misuse of Ancient Knowledge by evil magicians. At the time she had sensed it was a *warning*, and now she was certain. Whatever powers the Great Loogastric possessed, they were more than magical sleight of hand and innocent illusion. They had to do with ancient solemn rites, steeped in mystery, secrecy, and danger, and Loogastric was their evil exponent.

"Look at that guy," Jamie said admiringly. "I'll bet he has a great act."

Amy did not reply but continued to stare at the magician. Loogastric seemed far older than his physical years

28

implied . . . almost as ancient as the powers he possessed . . . in fact, *thousands* of years older than any living man. Amy sensed this so strongly, yet she knew the idea was ridiculous. Still, she could not take her eyes off the magician's face. For an instant Loogastric, as if aware of her gaze, stared back. From out of the hundreds of people in the crowd, he had selected her, and their eyes connected.

Petrified, Amy quickly turned away. She nudged Jamie. "Let's go home now, the parade is over."

"Go home, are you crazy?"

"There's nothing more to see," she argued.

The last of the circus wagons, elephants, and horses had now disappeared from sight, well on their way to the football field where the Fanzini Troupe would set up their tents for the week's performances.

"Listen," said Jamie, "I've been thinking over what you said and you're right. Books aren't the only source of information. I could do a great report on circus history by interviewing some of the performers. I'll bet the Fanzinis know all about circus history." Jamie was still feeling guilty about the way he had behaved the day before. "Whaddya say? Why don't we try to interview some of them for our report?"

"*Our* report?" Amy asked.

"Sure, we'll *share* the information—just as long as you write your own."

That was as close to an apology as Jamie would ever get, so Amy eagerly accepted. "Okay, it's a deal."

Chapter Five

WHEN THE TWINS ARRIVED AT THE FOOTBALL FIELD, THEY WIT-nessed an amazing sight. Nearly all the performers who earlier had marched down Main Street in jeweled costumes and sequined capes were now wearing jeans, sweatshirts, and overalls. Gone was the illusion of grandeur and splendor that they had created during the parade, but something equally fascinating was now taking place. Wire walkers, bareback riders, and clowns alike, all joined the roustabouts in the sweaty labor of erecting a transient circus city.

Elephants started pushing the trucks into position, beginning with the one equipped with the all-important stake-driving machine. Once the center poles were in place, the giant bales of canvas were laid on the ground and unrolled. Sledges slammed down on the stake to drive it into the ground. Then the troupe spread out the canvas sections, laced them together, and lashed the canvas to bail rings at the center poles. As if by magic, the tent suddenly took shape and was quickly raised.

Another truck carried an enormous generator that would create the special theatrical lighting effects. People bustled around, delivering stock feed to the menagerie and horse tent, and food to the bus-cookhouse.

Amy was amazed that in just a few days all these people would be miles away, in some other area of the countryside, repeating the same process.

Jamie was impressed by the organization and teamwork such a task must require. Everyone knew his job, and did it willingly.

Within two hours activity at the site had slowed down. As the twins strolled about watching the final bits of construction, they came upon a group of circus children playing a game of soccer outside one of the living trailers.

The boy Jamie had noticed during the parade kicked the ball high into the air, then turned to smile at him. "Hi. Coming to the show tonight?"

"Sure."

"My name's Gino, what's yours?"

"Jamie."

Hearing the clang of the lunch bell, Gino waved and ran toward the cookhouse. "Bye, Jamie, see you tonight."

Lorenza Fanzini, in a denim shirt and jeans, came hurrying from the cookhouse to gather the remaining children. Like a mother hen with her chicks, she hustled them together, shouting, "Get it while it's hot." Her robust voice told of her zest for life.

Armando Fanzini was busy supervising the last remaining details in the erecting of the big top, pointing and nodding his approval while loudly singing an operatic aria.

"Excuse me, Mr. Fanzini," Jamie said, "do you have a minute?"

"A minute?" he asked dramatically. "No, not a *second*. Tonight the Fanzinis shall perform. There may be glamour in the ring, but there's only sweat outside of it, and a hundred more things must be done."

"We're learning about circus history for school," Amy explained, "and we hoped we could interview you."

"Circus history?" Signore Fanzini let out a bellow of laughter. "I *am* circus history. Wherever there is a circus, there is a Fanzini."

"Yeah," Jamie said, "there seem to be a lot of you. How many Fanzinis are there exactly?"

"Only God knows that." He chuckled. "We are scattered over the face of the earth in many different circus troupes—cousins, second cousins, who can count?"

Lorenza Fanzini came hurrying toward her husband. "In your whole life you haven't had a hot meal, Papa. How can you perform if you don't eat?"

"I'll eat, Mama, don't worry. For forty years you've told me that, and for forty years I've eaten. But first I must speak to these children. They're studying circus history."

Madame Fanzini put her hands on her hips and gave a sigh of exasperation as well as acceptance: she would not, as her sigh implied, change one aspect of her husband's robust, generous, enthusiastic personality. "You want to know about the Fanzinis?" she asked.

32

The twins nodded.

"Then you'll learn about us over lunch," she declared. "You children look like you could use a good hot meal too. I'll have the cook serve up two more plates."

As Madame Fanzini hurried back to the cookhouse, her husband escorted the twins to the main trailer which served as the Fanzinis' living quarters while they were on the road.

Amy was surprised to see how homey things were inside. The beds, tables, and furniture were all small and compact, but there were stiffly starched curtains at the windows, and dozens of family pictures. There were even several vases of fresh spring flowers, and a home-made quilt was tacked on the wall.

"Mama likes things neat," Signore Fanzini explained proudly as he opened up the collapsible table attached to the wall underneath the window. He pulled up some chairs and invited the children to sit down. "I love the view from this window," he said.

Through the window the twins could see the wagons for the wild animals, and the horses being paraded by for their afternoon exercise.

Signore Fanzini took a linen cloth from a drawer and covered the small table. Then he folded four linen napkins and placed one by each plate. "Mama also likes things proper," he explained.

Lorenza Fanzini entered the trailer carrying a tray with four steaming plates of pasta covered in meat sauce and four tall glasses of milk. "First we eat, then we talk," she said.

Amy eagerly began her meal. The smell of hay, sawdust, and canvas wafted in through the open trailer door, and the sounds of lions, elephants, and horses could be heard in the background. All the tantalizing aromas and sensations of the circus seemed to become mingled inside the Fanzinis' cozy trailer, and Amy knew she was eating the most delicious dish of spaghetti she had ever tasted.

"It's good you must learn about circus history," said Madame Fanzini, placing a bowl of fresh fruit on the table. "Ours is a noble tradition. Papa's family performed in Europe hundreds of years ago. In those days there was always a Fanzini at a royal court."

"That's true," Signore Fanzini said. "My ancestor Cesare Fanzini was a clown tumbler in the court of Marie Antoinette. He was known as le Sauteur."

Jamie's French was very good, so he translated. "Doesn't that mean 'the leaper'?"

"Exactly. It was said Cesare could entertain the queen as no one else in France. In fact, he bore a letter with Marie Antoinette's royal seal which allowed him safe conduct when traveling. In those days being allowed to travel freely was always a problem for circus folk. Many considered us unrespectable."

"Another good reason you should know about our history," Madame Fanzini said firmly. "We are not thieves or gypsies. Our children work hard, do their schoolwork, and our families are very close. Circus families can't survive otherwise. We all count on one another's help, especially in the ring. The circus means teamwork."

"I know," Jamie said admiringly. "I couldn't believe how fast you got everything set up this morning."

Signore Fanzini nodded. "Precision and accuracy, that's

also what the circus means. And loyalty, of course. Together, our family can face any disaster."

"And we have," his wife added. "Even during the war the Fanzinis always performed."

"That's because we always had you, Mama."

Madame Fanzini blushed. "But now I'm just ringmaster—too old for the ring."

"Ah, but in your day"—her husband sighed, fondly remembering his wife's former glory—"you were the greatest rider from the noblest equestrian family in Europe."

"When did you stop riding?" Amy asked.

"Years ago. I was doing my bareback act—"

"A *wonderful* act," Signore Fanzini interjected. "Lorenza would dance a special ballet on the horse's back. Leaping through a hoop decorated with flowers, she would dance and pose, then finally do a double pass through the hoop. She'd toss the flowers to the spectators, then more horses would enter the ring and Lorenza would bounce from one to the other, horse to horse, ground to horse, horse to ground . . ."

"Until one horse stumbled and threw me," said Madame Fanzini with a note of finality.

"But you picked yourself up," her husband said in her defense. "You picked yourself up and made a gallant exit from the ring."

"And I never returned. It is always important to know when to *stop*, Papa." Lorenza stared at her husband meaningfully, as if that comment had been directed at him. "But my family continues," she added brightly. "My granddaughter, Maria, is now the *prima* bareback rider. My sons Emilio and Pietro work the high wire. Julio has

35

his lions, and the little ones are on trapeze and work with the ponies. I don't need to perform anymore."

Armando Fanzini began to laugh. "But you still crack the whip, Mama!"

"As ringmaster, yes, but *you* are still the boss, Papa."

Amy enjoyed listening to the Fanzinis' playful teasing. They were bound together by love and respect. The circus was their self-contained world, and they were proud of their place within it.

"I'd like to hear more about your act, Mr. Fanzini," said Jamie. "Have there been trapeze artists in your family for hundreds of years?"

Signore Fanzini curled his mustache between his fingers and smiled. "That would be impossible. Tumblers and leapers have performed for centuries, but the flying trapeze did not exist in the early days. It was invented by a Frenchman named Léotard in 1859."

"No kidding," Jamie said. "You mean those tights you all wear are named after a man?"

"An ingenious man, who in his day had many things named after him—everything was *à la Léotard*. When he performed in Paris, he had five trapezes in a line and turned somersaults from one to the next. No one had ever seen such a thing before. Yes, Léotard was one of the great ones."

Smiling to himself, Jamie took out his notebook and began writing down facts. Nelson Rappaport would probably have to read several books to learn that Léotard was actually a *man*. Jamie congratulated himself for having the terrific idea of interviewing *real* circus folk.

"At the height of Léotard's fame," Signore Fanzini concluded, "he died of smallpox."

"Which just goes to prove we're all human, Papa," said his wife as she cleared away the dishes. "We get sick, too, and we get *old*," she added firmly, "just like everyone else."

"But not as quickly, Mama," he argued, pounding his chest with his fist. "See, hard as a rock, every muscle. This is important, children. A tired muscle that does not respond quickly enough may mean instant death to an aerialist. That's why all the Fanzinis believe in clean living, healthy bodies—and no smoking or drinking."

"We also believe in knowing the names of our guests," said Madame Fanzini.

The twins began to laugh, realizing they had never properly introduced themselves, so they did.

"Well, Amy and Jamie," said Signore Fanzini, "have we given you enough information?"

"Oh, no," Jamie said, "there's lots more I want to know."

"Then you must come back another time. Maybe after the performance tonight."

"Could we?" Amy asked. The Fanzinis were such pleasant, friendly people, she already felt she had known them for ages.

Madame Fanzini nodded. "Of course you may."

Just then Gino came bursting into the trailer. "Can I practice my new act now, Grandma?"

"Not yet, Gino. Schoolwork first."

"But, Grandma—"

"Schoolwork first," repeated Lorenza Fanzini sternly. "First you exercise the brain, then the muscles."

"Okay," he grumbled, "but I'd rather balance on the high wire than do math any day!"

Amy laughed. "So would I! I've never been on a high wire but it can't be harder than math."

"Go," ordered Madame Fanzini. "Spend at least one hour with your schoolbooks, you hear?"

Gino grabbed a tangerine from the fruit bowl, then hurried out the door just as his sister, Maria, was entering.

Maria was a lovely young woman with long black hair tied tightly into a bun and with the same brilliantly green eyes as her grandmother. Amy felt she was probably a mirror image of Lorenza Fanzini some forty years earlier.

"Grandma, I need the key to the strongbox."

"The strongbox? You never wear the tiara during rehearsal."

"I know, but Vittorio says we should practice in full costume this afternoon," she explained.

"All right," said Madame Fanzini, taking a large set of keys from her jeans. As she was about to pull one off the ring, her husband grabbed her arm. "No, Mama, the tiara is only worn during performances. It is tradition and we must not break tradition."

Madame Fanzini nodded. "That's true, Papa. You must practice without the tiara, Maria. For two hundred years we have done things this way. I'll give you the key to the strongbox before the show."

"All right," agreed Maria. "Oh, Grandpa, Vittorio needs you to help check the perches and the wire setups for the pyramid."

Madame Fanzini's face turned pale. "The pyramid? Armando, you promised to cut that from the act."

"No, I never promised, Mama; I said I'd think about it."

"But you're too old for the pyramid," she argued. "Why must you tempt fate once again?"

As Amy listened to the Fanzinis argue the point, she realized this was a sensitive point of disagreement. Evidently the pyramid was a spectacular act, but also extremely dangerous.

Signore Fanzini refused to listen to his wife's misgivings. "Enough said, Mama. I will use a net tonight, I promise, but now I must help set things up."

Madame Fanzini threw up her hands in disgust as her husband and granddaughter left the trailer. "That man is so stubborn and thickheaded," she shouted after him. "Can you imagine? He thinks he's still a spring chicken when he's really an old bird too tough even for the stew pot!"

"We'd better go now," Jamie said. "Thanks for lunch and all the information."

Despite her anger, Madame Fanzini managed a smile. "You write good reports about the circus for school and you both come see us again."

The twins left the trailer, and Lorenza Fanzini hurried down the field toward the big top. Amy knew the argument between the fiery Fanzinis wasn't over yet!

The children passed Gino, who was seated at the side of the trailer. "Hi there," he said, obviously more interested in the passing elephants than in the math book on his lap. "You were talking to my grandparents a long time. What about?"

"Circus history," Amy said. "They told us lots of fascinating things."

Gino nodded. "Yeah, Grandma and Grandpa know lots about that. When Grandpa started out in Europe, all he had was a caravan and six starving horses."

"I'll bet you'd like to have your own circus someday too," Jamie said.

Gino closed his math book. "Maybe. But first I'd like to be the starring act in the Ringling Brothers circus. I've been flying since I was four, you know." Rick, one of the handlers, paraded the elephants by, and Gino asked, "Would you like to pet them?"

The twins nodded, and Amy approached one of the huge animals to stroke its gray hide. She jumped away as the elephant suddenly started bobbing its head and bouncing around. "Maybe it doesn't like me. All I did was pat it."

"Not that way," explained Gino, giving the elephant a firm slap on the back which instantly calmed it down. "See? They love a good slap, but a pat tickles their skin and drives them crazy."

Amy tried again. Both she and Jamie whacked the elephant's back. To their surprise, the animal seemed to enjoy it.

"That's right," Gino said. "Elephants may be big, but their skin is very sensitive."

As they walked over the grounds with Gino, Amy noticed the Great Loogastric's trailer in the distance, set apart from all the other living trailers. Painted across its side was a pyramid with an eye in the center and other strange mystical symbols. Instead of frilly curtains, dark drapes covered the windows.

Observing the trailer, Amy got the same frightening feeling she had had when she saw the magician in the parade. "Is Loogastric one of your family too?" she asked.

"Him?" Gino laughed, as if the idea were ridiculous. "No way. He's only been with us a little while. My mom always says all circus folk are family, but I don't like him."

"Why not?" Amy asked, anxious to know if Gino had the same unpleasant feeling about the man.

"I don't know. He keeps to himself all the time, and he never laughs. I think he's creepy." Gino picked up a pebble and threw it into the air. "He's not one of us, know what I mean? When we had the fire in the cookhouse, everyone helped put it out except Loogastric."

"What fire?" Jamie asked.

"Last week one of the butane gas tanks exploded just before a performance. We nearly had to cancel the show, but no one was hurt and we got the thing under control real fast. Grandpa said we were lucky it didn't frighten the animals. Anyway, Loogastric was the only one who didn't pitch in. He just sat in that trailer with the door locked." Gino threw a final pebble into the air. "Well, I've gotta go now. Look for me in the show tonight, okay? I'll be wearing red."

The twins waved good-bye as Gino ran in the direction of the big top.

Jamie sucked in a deep breath of spring air. "This has

41

been a great day, hasn't it? I can hardly wait to see the show tonight."

As they walked along the football field, leaving the tantalizing sights and smells of the makeshift circus city behind them, Amy grew thoughtful. Yes, it had been a great day, but . . . "Something awful is going to happen tonight, Jamie," she blurted out. "The Fanzinis are in danger."

Jamie stared at his sister. "Are you getting one of your weird psychic twitches again?"

"Yes. I don't know what's going to happen, but someone will be hurt. I think that magician, Loogastric, is—"

"Don't tell me," Jamie said sarcastically, "let me guess. He's actually an *evil* magician, right? He dabbles in black magic and plans to put a spell on someone."

"Maybe; I don't know. But yesterday Jeb warned me about evil magicians."

"I might've known," said Jamie, losing all patience with his sister. "Every time you get one of your cocka-mamy ideas, Jeb is involved. He must be nuttier than you are! I'll tell you one thing, I'm glad *I* never see him, and I never want to."

"Let's forget it," she snapped, and hurried ahead of her brother. She tried to push the disturbing thought from her mind and looked now at the bursts of yellow bloom on the forsythia bushes. She tried to follow Jamie's example and so did her best to look forward to the exciting opening of the circus that evening.

Yet somewhere inside a gnawing feeling told Amy that the delighted squeals of the audience would turn to tragic screams before the night was over.

And she was powerless to stop it!

Chapter Six

WITH NIGHTFALL THE CIRCUS GROUNDS TOOK ON A TRULY magical appearance. The outside of the big top was strung with colored lights, and the calliope music filled the air. Also wafting through the air were the sweet, buttery, and pungent scents from the concessions selling cotton candy, popcorn, and hot dogs. Clowns mingled with the crowd, which eagerly awaited the opening performance.

Madame Fanzini, in her capacity as ticket seller, was standing at the entrance to the big top collecting admission fees. She wore a tailored black satin jacket with sequined lapels, bright red satin riding britches, a bow tie, and a top hat.

"You're right, Jamie," his father agreed, "that's a very impressive-looking woman."

The twins quickly introduced their parents to Lorenza Fanzini. Despite the bustle around her, she took time to shake their hands. "Enjoy the show," she commanded, handing them their tickets.

The Fergusons entered the marquee and took their seats up front. Mr. Ferguson checked the program and noted that among the sideshow attractions was a ventriloquist, a performing seal, and a snake charmer named Salome. "Let's visit her booth after the show, Miriam."

Mrs. Ferguson grinned. "Do you think she knows Seraphina?"

"She might. Circus folk are very clannish."

"But you know what Thomas Wolfe said, Richard: 'You can't go home again.' "

"I don't accept Wolfe's statement, Miriam. In fact—"

A brassy flourish of trumpets interrupted Mr. Ferguson's argument: the grand entry parade was about to begin.

The back-door curtain of the tent snapped open, and the chatter and rustle of the audience died down with the dimming house lights. Madame Fanzini entered the center of the ring. She saluted first the audience and then the company, which began to parade before her. First came the grooms, each leading two plumed horses; a pretty girl in a silken costume followed on an elephant. Next came the band and, behind them, a varied procession of clowns, Shetland ponies, acrobats, and riders. More elephants appeared, this time riderless and in spangled blankets. They moved along trunk to tail, with their attendants plodding alongside. Then the tumblers and high-wire performers entered the ring.

Jamie spotted Gino in his red sequined cape and waved to him. Gino waved back at everyone in general and perhaps at Jamie in particular. Then came the Flying Fanzinis: two men and two women, proudly led by Armando Fanzini in a sparkling white leotard.

As the entry parade completed its circle around the ring, Amy noticed that the Great Loogastric was not part of the ensemble.

Madame Fanzini quickly took up her station, where she would announce and control the evening's performance. She blew her whistle, cracked her whip in the air, and declared the first attraction would be Julio and His Amazing Lions.

The crowd roared louder than the animals as the cages were wheeled out. The connecting chutes, fastened end to end, were then opened. The crack of whiplashes resounded as Julio, dressed in a safari outfit and pith helmet, put the wild beasts through their paces. On his command, they balanced balls, stood on pedestals, and leapt through flaming hoops, all to the delight of the eager spectators.

Julio's act was followed by the rope walkers; then a comical ballet was performed by children, dogs, and Shetland ponies.

There was definitely no shortage of acts in the Fanzinis' one-ring circus enterprise. Next came foot jugglers, and a charming baby elephant act, followed by some of the Fanzini grandchildren performing on the fixed trapeze. Naturally, the twins applauded extra loudly for Gino, who executed several intricate bar tricks and passes.

Next came Maria Fanzini and her marvelous equestrian act. She wore a magnificent pink spangled skirt, cross-gartered ballet shoes, and a sparkling tiara. Her jeweled crown glistened underneath the spotlights as Maria and her company performed amazing tricks. Standing on the broad quarters of her rosinback horse with ankles crossed and toes pointed, she suddenly turned a forward somersault with a half-twist. Then she leapt through paper hoops and blew kisses to her delighted audience. Leaping with lightning speed, she somersaulted from one horse to another, constantly quickening her pace.

As Amy watched Maria she pictured the young Lorenza Fanzini performing similar acts of skill many years earlier. Amy also thought of her own mother, who had fantasized about becoming a bareback rider. For an instant she, too, wished she could run away and join the circus.

Maria's act climaxed when her brother Lucio entered the ring. He was disguised as a ragged drunk. Staggering between the horses, he struggled to mount one, at which point Maria somersaulted from her horse onto his shoulders, then waved farewell to the crowd as she left the ring.

At the end of Maria's performance the applause continued until Madame Fanzini once again blew her whistle. "And now," she announced, "we are pleased to present for your edification and amazement the Great Loogastric, grand master of illusion and legerdemain, with powers learned in the ancient capitals of the world."

The kettledrum rolled, the spotlights faded until the arena was almost in darkness, and all was quiet as Loogastric entered the ring. With a wave of his hand he created a fiery flame that burned in midair above his head.

47

The audience gasped, and Madame Fanzini calmed their fears: "Do not panic, this is merely an illusion. Please allow the Great Loogastric to continue."

The crowd settled down, and Loogastric proceeded. The audience was now in the palm of his hand. Having suspended their notions of reality, they gave themselves over to his compelling illusions.

One fantastic image followed another. Loogastric's sleight-of-hand tricks included changing colored scarves into what appeared to be a rushing waterfall of rainbow colors. With a sword he severed an assistant's head in full view of the audience. The head was then placed on a platter, and as the astounded crowd watched, it magically reappeared upon the victim's shoulders. By means of a magic lantern Loogastric projected the images of ghostly figures onto smoke. Then he set a dozen doves on fire, and flames seemed to consume their bodies. Suddenly the birds, miraculously intact, rose to the top of the tent and fluttered above the audience.

Jamie couldn't believe his eyes. He had seen many magicians perform, but Loogastric created effects far superior to any rabbit-out-of-the-hat tricks. With the mere wave of his hand lightning bolts careered from one end of the tent to the other. Strange unearthly shapes seemed to appear within the arena, then disappeared just as quickly. "This guy is great, Dad. How does he do it?"

"I don't know," admitted Mr. Ferguson, equally impressed. "It's probably a combination of mathematics, optics, and physics."

Amy did not agree. As the rest of the audience enjoyed what they considered to be carefully constructed magical illusions, she felt they were actually witnessing true *sorcery*. Loogastric's secret powers enabled him actually to do the things he merely appeared to be doing.

Throughout his act Loogastric never spoke. His actions alone, his every move, riveted the audience. For his finale he raised both his hands overhead and, as if chan neling power from heaven itself, suddenly disappeared. Without the aid of magical boxes or concealing curtains, Loogastric was gone!

Once again the arena was empty. The audience, silent for a moment, broke into boisterous applause for the magician's final and most spectacular trick.

But Loogastric did not return to take a bow.

Instead, Madame Fanzini announced the last act of the evening. "And now the Flying Fanzinis will perform their famous pyramid on the high wire. This feat requires precision, technique, and split-second timing. Ladies, gentlemen, and children, we request your silent attention." She raised her hand, and the spotlight focused on the five Fanzinis, positioned on their perches beside the high wire suspended one hundred feet above the ground.

The Fanzinis began their performance with several midflight releases from the trapeze. While in midair, Yolanda Fanzini combined various twists and somersaults, then returned to her catcher, brother Enrico. Then came several double passes with all the flyers performing their movements with the precision of ballet dancers. For an instant, two figures could be seen flying through the air in opposite directions, one above the other.

The Fanzinis were the best trapeze act Jamie had ever seen. He now understood better what Signore Fanzini

49

CHESTER PUBLIC LIBRARY
CHESTER, ILLINOIS

had told him about teamwork, and he eagerly awaited the finale of the act, the famous pyramid. For this trick two more aerialists joined the high wire. The four men walked along the wire, linked in pairs by bars hooked over their shoulders. On each of the two bars stood a middleman; the two middlemen were also linked by a bar. On top of this bar, Yolanda Fanzini, the top mounter, balanced precariously on a chair. The seven aerialists created a spectacular body pyramid which seemed to defy gravity.

But the cheers of the crowd suddenly turned to frightened screams as the delicately composed structure began to collapse. One of the aerialists at the bottom of the pyramid lost his balance, causing all of them to sway back and forth on the high wire. As the structure began to crumble, all seven frantically grasped onto the wire and hung there precariously. All of them managed to maintain their hold, except for Armando Fanzini, who fell into the net suspended beneath him. He quickly picked himself up and waved to the audience to assure them he had not been injured. But Amy noticed he limped from the arena. Perhaps he had not been hurt badly, but he had definitely been injured.

Madame Fanzini, a true showman and trouper, tried to disguise her concern as she announced the show's conclusion: "Anyone who missed the sideshow and menagerie of wild animals will have another chance to see it now." Then she hurried toward the exit. Amy knew she was rushing to her trailer to learn about her husband's condition.

"Thank goodness they used a net in their act," said Mrs. Ferguson.

Her husband agreed. "I've never seen that trick done before, but several aerialists have died trying it."

Amy glanced at her brother. She had told him something awful would happen, and it had. Jamie did not acknowledge her glance; he was always uneasy when one of his sister's peculiar predictions came true.

The unexpectedly dramatic conclusion of the show had, naturally, filled the audience with concern. But that potential danger inherent in all circus performances had also given the crowd an extra edge of excitement. On leaving the big top, many were eager to maintain that excitement and so strolled the grounds and visited the sideshows.

Mr. Ferguson was anxious to check out the snake charmer Salome. Amy and Jamie were more concerned about Signore Fanzini's injury.

"Okay," said their father, "we'll all meet back by the exit in half an hour."

As the twins hurried toward the elder Fanzinis' trailer, Amy received another premonition: This was only the first of the many circus accidents soon to befall the Fanzinis!

Chapter Seven

"Stop it!" protested Armando Fanzini. "You're treating me like a baby."

Madame Fanzini was holding an ice pack in one hand and a steaming hot towel in the other. As her husband lay on the sofa, she applied them alternately to his bruised ankle. Their sons Julio and Enrico and granddaughter Yolanda were all seated beside their father. "Why so much fuss?" he shouted. "I'm not dying."

"No thanks to you," Lorenza shouted back. "I told you to cut the pyramid from the act, Papa. Those old legs of yours won't do what you command any longer."

"It wasn't my legs," he argued, "it was the equipment. Fatigue in the metal must've caused the apparatus to snap."

"No, Father," Enrico said, "we checked everything before the performance, remember?"

Signore Fanzini refused to believe that his age was the sole cause of his accident. "Then the ground level was off," he said.

"Maybe you should check your equipment again," Amy suggested. She was reluctant to interfere in what was clearly a family matter. Yet, if it were possible to prevent what she feared might be a string of similar accidents, she felt compelled to speak up.

"That's right," Jamie said. "My sister has an instinct about things like this." To Amy's relief, he stopped short of revealing she was psychic.

Madame Fanzini also agreed. "Yes, Enrico, check everything again. We must prove to your father that destiny has spoken."

Madame Fanzini was still very upset, yet she also seemed strangely resigned about her husband's accident. As with her own career in the ring, she felt fate had stepped in to tell him it was time to retire.

After Enrico and his brother had left the trailer, Madame Fanzini offered the twins some tea. "It was nice of you to stop by, children."

"Well, they haven't come to see an old man on his *deathbed*," grumbled Armando. He attempted to stand up, but by now his ankle had swollen to twice its normal size.

Madame Fanzini banged four cups onto the table. "Sit down, Papa!"

Jamie felt like an intruder. "Maybe we'd better go."

"No, don't leave, I need protection from this old woman's sharp tongue," said Signore Fanzini. He had no fear

53

of the high wire but felt helpless in the face of his wife's anger. "Just sit and wait. When Enrico returns, we'll discover who's right."

"And who's wrong," his wife added.

The tension mounted inside the trailer, and the twins sipped their tea in silence. After a while Enrico returned to inform his father that he had scrupulously double-checked every piece of flying equipment and had discovered that one of the cable wires was broken. "I can't understand it, Father. We checked everything before the performance."

Signore Fanzini was thrilled. "I knew my legs weren't to blame. That settles it, Mama; as soon as this ankle is healed I will fly again!"

Madame Fanzini threw up her hands in disgust.

As the Fanzinis continued to argue, Amy grew more and more concerned about the couple. Each one was so obviously dedicated to the other's welfare. But, she realized, they were both missing an important factor regarding the accident:

If the equipment had been checked earlier, the cable wire must have been deliberately cut just before the performance—cut by someone who wanted to hurt the Fanzinis!

As the twins left the trailer, Amy was reluctant to share her concerns with her brother. Jamie was always accusing her of imagining things that she knew were actually revelations. Besides, she had no evidence, and Jamie worshiped concrete, irrefutable *facts*; so she decided to keep silent.

When they met their parents in front of the big top, the children noticed that their father looked strangely preoccupied.

"What's wrong, Dad?" Jamie asked.

"Your father just had a major disappointment," said Mrs. Ferguson. From the tone of her voice they realized she must be teasing.

"What happened?" Amy asked. "Didn't you get to meet Salome?"

Mr. Ferguson did not reply.

"Oh, we met her," Mrs. Ferguson explained. "In fact, we all had a nice long talk."

Jamie did not understand. "So what's wrong? Doesn't she know Seraphina?"

Mr. Ferguson was still silent, deep in thought.

"Oh, she knows her very well," said Mrs. Ferguson. "Salome visited her last winter. It seems Seraphina and her serpents did quite well for themselves. She saved all her money, and after her pythons died, she retired to a pig farm in Wisconsin. Salome said she still has all her teeth, even though she's seventy-five years old."

Mr. Ferguson sighed. "I just never thought she'd grow *old*, Miriam. Maybe Tom Wolfe was right: you *can't* go home again."

"Don't take it so hard, dear." His wife grinned. "By now Bruno the Lion Tamer probably has no teeth at all!"

Mr. Ferguson did take it hard. The realization that his Superwoman was no longer young, and that her pythons were no longer living, seemed a symbolic tolling of the death knell for his own lost youth. Richard Ferguson no longer considered himself young enough to run away and join the circus as his fellow professor had done six years earlier. He was now permanently stuck in the life of academia he had constructed around himself. All fantasies of escape must now be a thing of the past.

In his own way Jamie was in a funk, too. What did he really have going for himself? he asked. Amy's psychic abilities were far more intriguing; Gino's life on the trapeze was far more fascinating. And no matter how hard he tried, Nelson Rappaport's project would probably be far more interesting. All Jamie had was an analytical mind which might someday be replaced by a *computer*. Hardly a great future!

He was so depressed, he wasn't certain he wanted to return to the circus the next night.

"Why not?" Amy asked. "I bet they'll have lots of different acts tonight."

Amy did not tell her brother the real reason she wanted to return: During the performance someone else's life would be in danger. If she was there when it happened, she could do something about it.

"Go along with Amy," insisted Mrs. Ferguson. "I think you children should go *every* night. After all, you're only young once."

That comment did not serve to lighten Richard Ferguson's mood. "Your mother's right," he said solemnly. "As the poet said: 'Gather ye rosebuds while ye may, / Old Time is still a-flying.' " He sighed deeply and walked dramatically toward the kitchen door; then whispered the end of the quote as he slowly left the room: " 'And this same flower that smiles today / Tomorrow will be dying.' "

"Hey, Mom," Jamie said, "what's wrong with Dad?"

Mrs. Ferguson shook her head. "It's nothing serious, children. Go to the circus and have fun."

Chapter Eight

ONCE AGAIN THE FANZINI TROUPE HAD A PACKED HOUSE.

The lighthearted enthusiasm of all the performers in no way suggested the near disaster that had occurred the night before. Circus folk were accustomed to living on the edge of danger and always took it in their stride.

As with all live performances, one is never the same as another. That potential for change, perfection, or disaster kept the audience on the edge of their seats just as it had the night before.

During Julio's opening act with his lions, the twins noticed that the animals seemed particularly surly and hard to manage; but Maria's act with her rosinback horses got even more applause than it had the previous evening. Amy thought she looked just like a princess as she somersaulted through the air. She landed as delicately as a snowflake on the horse's hindquarters, her gleaming tiara glistening beneath the stage lights.

The Great Loogastric created totally different illusions, and all were as impressive as the ones they had already seen.

The pyramid had been cut from the trapeze act, and now Madame Fanzini announced that Enrico would perform his specialty. "He will spring over five elephants, side by side—a leap of forty feet complete with a double twist and somersault as he flies through the air."

The audience watched eagerly as the elephants were lined up in position and the padded mattresses laid down on the sawdust. As the drums rolled, Enrico hurled himself into the air. For an instant it seemed he was suspended above the giant pachyderms, then he twisted his body around in preparation for his descent.

But something went wrong, which threw Enrico's timing off. As he missed the final twist his shoulder smashed against the back of the fifth elephant, and he fell limply onto the mattress. He lay there, obviously in pain, until two attendants ran into the ring and helped carry him toward the exit.

But the ringmaster did not skip a beat. Madame Fanzini quickly introduced the next act, and the ring was soon filled with barrels of monkeys, supervised by their trainer, Claudio.

Amy did not pay attention to the rest of the show. She was now convinced that every member of the Fanzini family was in imminent danger. Some evil force seemed bent upon their destruction. She could not wait to get back to the trailers to discover how badly Enrico had been injured.

*　　*　　*

"I hope the Fanzinis don't think we're snooping," said Amy as she and Jamie walked between the rows of parked trailers, "but I'm really worried about Enrico."

The twins noticed Gino in the distance. He was walking toward them. No longer wearing his performance clothes, he carried a thermos and an ice pack. They hurried along to catch up with him.

"How's your uncle?" Amy asked.

"He sprained his shoulder pretty badly. I guess he and Grandpa will both be out of the show for a while."

"You guys are certainly in a dangerous business," Jamie said.

"I guess so, but my uncle has done that trick hundreds of times. Nothing ever happened before." Gino paused, reluctant to share family problems with outsiders. "Things have been pretty weird around here lately," he finally confessed. "Ever since— "

"Since Loogastric arrived?" Amy asked.

"Yeah," the boy admitted, "that's when all this hard-luck stuff began happening."

"What hard-luck stuff?" Jamie asked.

"Never mind," said Gino, regretting that he had brought up the subject. "Mom says circus problems should remain inside the circus; that's how we survive. Besides, I've got to get this ice pack over to my uncle's trailer."

"Give him our best," Amy said as Gino hurried away.

"What were you driving at just now?" Jamie asked. "You aren't serious about this evil magician nonsense, are you?"

"You heard what Gino said. Enrico never hurt himself

doing that trick before, so I wonder why it happened tonight?''

The activity under the big top was over for the night, and the audience around the sideshows had all gone home. But the circus grounds were still bustling with movement. Workmen were carrying bales of hay to the horses; coffee was being brewed in the bus-cookhouse; jugglers were practicing outside their trailers; and a baby lion was being walked along the grounds on a leash.

Off in the distance there was a strange rhythmic jingling like the eerie chimes of bells: a peculiarly haunting sound.

A clown, still in makeup, spotted the children. ''You shouldn't be here,'' he said. ''Nighttime near the big top is just for circus folk. What're you doing here?''

''Just looking around,'' said Jamie. ''What's that strange sound?''

''Creepy, isn't it?'' said the clown. ''It's them elephants shaking their shackles. They always do that when they're upset. Enrico's accident got them all nerved up. No one knows who gave 'em the water, ya see. That's what messed up the trick.''

''What water?'' Amy asked.

The clown acquired a real grin underneath his false smile. ''Letting them elephants drink before a performance is forbidden; any rookie knows that. Them bulls can take in more'n forty gallons at a time. It makes 'em swell up two feet and throws the whole trick off.''

''Who would've given them water?'' Jamie asked.

''Who knows? This used to be a great troupe for Joeys

like me, but everybody's got beefs lately. Nothin's gone right this season."

"What do you mean?" Amy asked.

Light from the overhead lamppost struck the man's clown-white makeup, turning him into a ghostly apparition. "Just what I said, girlie," he whispered. He grinned again, then ducked out of sight behind one of the trailers.

"What a creepy guy," observed Jamie, "and what a sick sense of humor. What's wrong with everyone around here? Why won't they talk to us?"

"They're afraid," Amy said. Tradition, she realized, had made circus folk as mystic as a cult. They had created their own world and fiercely protected it from the outside world; they were unwilling to share their problems. But Amy sensed that the present problem was far more serious than they suspected.

As the twins passed by the big top, they noticed an old man seated on a stool. He was wearing baggy overalls and an old felt hat with a hatband that held several lengths of coarse waxed cord and heavy needles. He had a worn canvas bag full of more cord and more needles in a block of wax, and in his belt he carried a long knife. By the muted light from the trailers he was busily patching a rip near the edge of the canvas.

The man looked up as the twins approached. His weather-beaten face told of many seasons spent on the road. He nodded at the children. "They call me the sailmaker," he said solemnly. "When I was younger, I used to do this by daylight. But now these old eyes are at half-mast all the time, so daylight and moonlight seem much the same. Why are you young ones wandering around so late?"

"We wanted to find out about Enrico," Amy explained. "We were worried."

The old man nodded. "Everyone worries after a fall. But worrying does no good. When our time comes, we must go."

A loud roar from the lions' cages pierced the silence of the circus grounds. "The cats are restless tonight," he observed. "Those beasts know more than we think they do. They see and they know," he repeated cryptically.

In the distance a light switched on inside Loogastric's trailer. Amy noticed this, as did the old man, who glanced toward the trailer, then shook his head and continued stitching the canvas with his callused fingers. "Like the Bible says, 'By their fruits ye shall know them.' But it's late now, young ones, you'd better go."

Jamie agreed. "Does everyone around here talk in riddles?" he asked. Without the lights, music, and performers, the circus grounds had an ominous, mysterious aspect, and he felt uneasy. "C'mon," he said, tugging at Amy's arm, "you found out what you wanted to know; Enrico is okay."

Amy, too, sensed that an ominous presence surrounded the big top, yet she felt strangely drawn to Loogastric's trailer; as if something compelled her to approach it.

"Don't go bothering him too," Jamie said. "Everyone's made it clear they don't want us hanging around. Let them solve their own problems."

"They can't," Amy argued, "they don't have the power."

"And you do, I suppose? C'mon, let's go."

Despite her brother's protests, Amy drew nearer to the Great Loogastric's trailer. The three-dimensional pyramid painted across its side caught Amy's attention, and held it. She knew that through the shifting sands of time the pyramid had been the symbol for eternity itself, its construction was steeped in ancient rites and mysteries. As those passing sands of time buried many civilizations, the pyramid had remained, a testament to their existence. It meant resurrection and rejuvenation—the gateway to all that is eternal.

The all-seeing eye in the center of the pyramid seemed to radiate power. Several smaller mystical symbols surrounded the pyramid: a pentagram, a magical sword, a Tree of Life, and a phoenix rising from flames.

"Kind of garish, isn't it?" Jamie noted. He would have preferred a snappy drawing of a tuxedoed magician carrying a rabbit and a top hat.

"They're ancient symbols," Amy explained, "and very powerful."

"Since when did you become an expert?"

"I don't know," she admitted. Something deep within Amy had made a connection with the symbols—something from another time; another life, perhaps.

As the twins stood beside the trailer, they became aware of a sudden silence. All activity at the circus grounds had come to a standstill. The elephants had ceased clanging their chains, the lions had ceased their roaring, and even the night sounds of nature had become abruptly muted.

A pungently sweet smell of incense wafted through the air as the Great Loogastric threw open his door. A lamp burned inside the trailer, and in its light the figure of the magician was silhouetted in the doorway. His feet were bare, and he wore a long white linen robe. Even in the half-light Amy felt the magnetic pull of his dark, piercing eyes.

Slowly Loogastric descended the trailer steps and approached the children. "Which of you seeks to know my powers," he asked, "and which of you questions them?" There was anger and arrogance in the magician's voice as he physically confronted the children.

Jamie immediately backed off. "I've got no questions, mister; I loved your act. I just thought I'd come by and— well, let you know."

Loogastric scoffed and turned away from Jamie, as if he had been speaking to an idiot. Then he stared at Amy. "You are the one," he said, pointing an accusing finger. "That face in the crowd; yes, I recognize your eyes. You seek to prevent me from pursuing my mighty path to glory." A faint, cold smile of recognition crossed Loogastric's face. "You are more than you appear to be, child. Yes," he continued, "I can see you are initiated into the first principles. You have much power for one so young." Amy knew that the magician could see far beyond the limits of ordinary comprehension. As he stared into her eyes, he was actually examining the depths of her being. "You have harnessed the forces around you," he added. "They are benign forces, but not without their power."

Amy stood motionless. The night air suddenly became hot and dry. The ground beneath her feet felt as if it had been baking in the hot sun—the arid Egyptian sun, aeons older than the pyramids.

Loogastric drew closer, then raised his hand to her forehead, and made the sign of a serpent. Then he began to chant: "In herbis, in verbis, et in lapidibus!" With a dark, disapproving scowl he thrust his chin forward and declared, "The Grand Copt himself stands before you; possessor of the Elixir of Life, older than the ages and more powerful." There was wrath in his blazing, pitiless eyes and rage in his voice as he continued: "Do not attempt to enter the magic circle, lest you be consumed by the fire. Only I and the phoenix shall rise from the ashes. O Darkness of the Ages, hear me: Let no one attempt to circumvent my just cause!" Loogastric made another mystical sign in the air, then he raised his arms above his head. "Acharat has spoken," he proclaimed to the darkness. "Revenge shall be my harvest." Then he ascended the steps of the trailer, slammed the door behind him, and was gone as quickly as he had appeared.

Jamie stood staring, his mouth hanging open. "That guy's got to be the world's biggest wacko. I think show biz has gone to his head."

"No, he's not crazy," Amy said, "he's dangerous. Couldn't you feel his power? Didn't you sense his vibrations?"

"Sure, I got his bad vibes; he's a sicko. Why else would he threaten you? You've never even met the guy."

"I'm not sure," Amy said. "I think I need to talk to Jebediah about this."

As the twins hurried from the circus grounds, Amy ripped one of the posters from a lamppost by the entrance and tucked it under her arm.

Chapter Nine

Jamie was depressed and disgusted, but he refused to admit that to Amy. He had always *hated* the ritual surrounding her contacts with Jeb, when she would drag out the candlesticks and try to summon him. Each time she did, it was another reminder that Amy had powers he could not begin to understand.

That night was no different. In her darkened room Amy lit the ancestral silver candlesticks, propped the poster beside them, then sat cross-legged on the floor.

Jamie stood in the doorway, deciding whether to leave or stay. "I think I'll go to bed," he said.

"Why?"

"Why not? I never see this ghost, I never hear him. *You're* the one with all the big-dealy powers!"

"I always tell you what Jeb says. Besides, he's our spirit guide, and he's dedicated to helping *both* of us; he told me so."

"Some guide," Jamie grumbled. "I could fall over him and not know it."

"Stop being negative," Amy argued. "I'll never get through to Jeb if you fill the room with negative energy."

"Coming from someone who always fails science, that comment is quite amusing."

"Well, at least shut up!" she shouted. "I'm trying to concentrate."

Jamie shuffled toward a corner chair as Amy closed her eyes and lowered her head. He would try thinking positively, he told himself. After all, it had saved Tinker Bell in *Peter Pan*, so maybe it could do something for him too. And after all, he *did* believe in Jeb—even though the guy didn't have the decency to introduce himself properly. And after all— Well, he would try to get into the "spirit" of the thing.

Amy began speaking softly. "Jebediah Aloysious Tredwell, please come visit us. We have questions and we need your help."

There was no movement in the room—no sound.

"Jeb," she continued, "I know you're always near us. Please appear."

A slight breeze blew through the open window, causing the candle flames to flicker. Two wisps of smoke rose from the flame. As they joined together in midair, they formed themselves into the ephemeral shape of Lieutenant Colonel Tredwell. "I am here, Cousin, attend my coming. What new intrigue have you upon your hands?"

Jamie was stunned. As usual he could not see the spirit; only this time he thought he heard something. The muffled voice was vague and faraway, like a radio signal that wasn't tuned in clearly, but it was definitely a voice. "Amy, I know Jeb is here. I mean I really know it. I can *hear* him."

Jebediah put his hands on his hips, thrust out his chest, and began to laugh. "Congratulations, lad. You possess a brilliant brain, but I suspect you have discovered that logic alone is too dry a food to live upon. Indeed, a most valuable lesson. But, Cousin, why have you called me to your bedchamber? I fear it must be for reasons of great magnitude."

Amy glanced at her brother. "Can you really hear what Jeb is saying?"

"Sure I can, honest," he assured her. "Jeb just said something about eating dried food in bed, right?"

"Not quite," Amy replied.

Jeb tried to clarify things. "My language speaks for itself, lad; do not adulterate the content of my words." Leaning over, he whispered into Amy's ear: "In truth, James hears but little and understands less. But with perseverance, his perceptions will increase."

Despite his limited perceptions, Jamie was thrilled. He jumped from the chair and paced the room excitedly. "This is terrific. I'm listening to a guy who's been dead for over two hundred years! Can you believe it? I mean, it puts the whole idea of science and physics in a new light. Absolutely terrific!"

"Calm yourself, Cousin," Jebediah ordered. "Be a friend to order and hasten to reveal your present distress."

"What'd he say?" Jamie asked. "Does Jeb want to order a meal?"

"He wants us to get to the point," Amy explained impatiently. "He hasn't got all night."

"Sure," Jamie said, sitting down beside his sister. "Hurry up and fill him in. Tell him all that junk you told me about Loogastric being evil."

"He *is* evil, Jeb," Amy said. "The Great Loogastric is a magician with the Fanzini Troupe. Since he arrived, awful things have been happening in the circus and I think he's caused them all, but I don't know why."

Jebediah listened carefully, then nodded. "I see, Cousin. You suspect this exponent of legerdemain is involved in more than innocent subterfuge?"

Amy nodded.

"Is it possible you fear he has unlocked the ancient mysteries and stolen from the Tree of Knowledge those fruits which are called the Elixir of Life? Is this not so?"

"Personally," said Jamie, "I think the guy has a great act. But he's also a major nut case. Maybe he believes his own advertising."

Jebediah pointed at the circus poster propped against the wall. "Perhaps you would be best advised to believe it as well. Do not scoff at that which you do not comprehend," he cautioned.

"What's that mean?" Jamie asked. "Are you telling us this guy *is* evil? Has he got black magic powers, or what?"

"You must be guided toward your own revelations, James. As in all things, each of us creates our own reality, our own illusion. Ignore this and my counsels are useless. I illuminate the path before you but can do no more. I suggest you examine that poster word by word—

70

letter by letter. Both mystery and solution may be revealed therein."

Having delivered his cryptic message, Jebediah suddenly vanished.

Amy was as puzzled as she had been before. But Jamie was far from confused; he was elated. He had finally heard Jebediah Tredwell speak! True, the message the spirit had given seemed a mystery, but it was one Jamie was determined to unravel.

He grabbed the poster and read it:

LOOGASTRIC, THE GRAND COPT, WITH
POWERS LEARNED FROM ANCIENT EGYPT

"There must be a clue here somewhere," he said excitedly. He switched on the light and grabbed a pad and pen from the desk. "The words could be in code," he reasoned. "Maybe it's a cipher."

Jamie had read several books on ciphers, so he tested out the theory. He began with a simple one, substituting various letters: *a* for *n* and *n* for *a*, and so on, but the letters created an unintelligible muddle. Next he changed the letters into numbers which stood for corresponding letters, but that didn't work either.

Amy continued to stare at the poster. "I don't think it's a cipher, Jamie; it's something else. Don't you think the name Loogastric is awfully odd? I mean, it doesn't sound real."

"You think it's phony?"

"It could be a stage name."

"Or a name within a name," Jamie concluded. "That's it, I'll bet it's an *anagram*."

Jamie quickly cut up several pieces of paper, printed one letter on each, and then rearranged them in various ways. No arrangement of letters seemed to spell anything until he came up with CALIOGROTS. Seeing this, Amy switched a few letters to spell CAGLIOSTRO. "I've heard that name before," she said, trying to remember where. "I think it was in a history book. Yes, and Jeb mentioned it too!"

"Then that's it," said Jamie. "The Great Loogastric may actually be Cagliostro."

"Sure, but who's *he?*"

"Beats me. But if he has anything to do with history, Dad will probably know. Let's ask him in the morning."

Chapter Ten

THE NEXT MORNING MR. FERGUSON WAS SEATED ON THE porch rocking chair watching the mailman make deliveries—and also watching the world pass by. Normally, during college recess Richard Ferguson would have a dozen household projects lined up, but at present he was still mourning his lost youth (and driving his wife crazy in the process!). So Miriam Ferguson was grateful when she overheard her children's question. Perhaps it would help to take their father's mind off his depression.

"Hey, Dad," Jamie said, "who's Cagliostro?"

"Doesn't he have something to do with history?" Amy said.

"Everything has something to do with history." Mr. Ferguson sighed, fully aware of his children's general uninterest in his field of knowledge. "Why do you ask? Another school project?"

73

"No," Jamie said, "we're just curious. Have you ever heard of him?"

"Of course. Most historians feel Cagliostro's involvement in the Affair of the Diamond Necklace sparked the beginning of the French Revolution; and it definitely caused Marie Antoinette's downfall."

The twins stared at each other, remembering what Armando Fanzini had told them. His ancestor Cesare had performed for Marie Antoinette! Could there possibly be some connection?

Jamie doubted it. "I don't think we're talking about the same guy, Dad. If he lived two hundred years ago, he couldn't still be around now."

Mr. Ferguson was growing more interested in the conversation. "That's an intriguing idea, Son. You see, Cagliostro was a famous magician and alchemist. He claimed he'd discovered the philosophers' stone, which held the secret of immortality."

Amy recalled the words both Jebediah and Loogastric had used the night before. "The Elixir of Life?"

"That's right," her father said. "Supposedly the stone not only has the power to transmute base metals into gold but can also rejuvenate the human body. Many of Cagliostro's patrons insisted they'd seen him change metals into pure gold before their eyes. They also swore he was thousands of years old."

"No kidding," said Jamie, "and people believed it?"

"They certainly did. Nowadays I guess Cagliostro would be called a confidence man, but in the eighteenth century people were very quick to believe his claims. To them, science and magic were one and the same. Cagliostro

74

called himself the Grand Copt and traveled through the major capitals of the world recruiting followers. Royalty was very impressed by him. He gave séances, foretold the future, and supposedly cured illnesses. In return, his patrons showered him with gifts and invited him to their palaces."

"He sounds like a deadbeat," Jamie said.

Mr. Ferguson shrugged. "Maybe; most historians consider him a charlatan, but I think he probably had some innate powers which he exaggerated. Unfortunately, he was arrogant, conceited, and overconfident. If he hadn't been, maybe his career wouldn't have been totally ruined by the Affair of the Diamond Necklace."

Mrs. Ferguson leaned out the kitchen window. "Lemonade, anyone?"

"Not now," said Jamie. "Dad's telling us a story and he's about to get to the good part."

Mr. Ferguson glanced at his wife suspiciously. "Did you send the kids out here to shake me out of my mood?"

"Certainly not, Richard. They're obviously interested in your story."

"That's right, Dad," Amy said. "Tell us about the diamond necklace."

"Diamonds?" Mrs. Ferguson asked. "I think *I'd* like to hear this too."

"Yeah, Dad," Jamie said, "tell us all about this guy."

By now Mr. Ferguson had also become enthusiastic. "Really? Would everyone like to hear it?" His wife and children nodded. "Okay, then let's adjourn to the kitchen for lemonade and some of your mom's delicious gingersnaps. A good story always sounds better with a snack!"

*   *   *

The Fergusons munched noisily on cookies as Mr. Ferguson began. "I should start by explaining that dozens of books have been written about the Affair of the Diamond Necklace. In every history of France it occupies at least a chapter. Napoleon himself regarded it as one of the causes of the French Revolution."

"Don't be so academic, dear," his wife said. "Just get to the good part."

"I'm giving the children the historical background, Miriam," explained her husband. "History is like a well-oiled machine, each cog helps move the other—no part of the mechanism is isolated. You have to understand there was great dissatisfaction and unrest in France. Both peasants and Parliament were tired of the excesses of their monarchy."

"We get the message, dear," said his wife. "Whose necklace caused all the trouble?"

Mr. Ferguson was now in his element. "Aha, that's the big question, and the source of all the controversy. There were lots of conflicting opinions about that."

Just as Amy was thinking her father would never get around to the good part, he finally did.

"The year was 1784," he began. "As I explained, Cagliostro was considered the wonder boy of the French court. He was also a close friend of Cardinal de Rohan, who had dreams of becoming a statesman. But at the time, Rohan wasn't in Marie Antoinette's favor. He'd infuriated her by gate-crashing a party she held at the Petit Trianon. In return, the queen refused to receive him at court."

"So far, this sounds like a fairy tale," Jamie commented.

"It's a bit spicier than that, Son. This is when Countess de La Motte-Valois enters the picture. She was what I'd call an adventuress. You might refer to her as a . . ."

"Shady lady?" Mrs. Ferguson suggested.

"Precisely. Very shady and very clever. She knew Rohan sought the queen's favor, so she convinced him she was a dear friend of Marie Antoinette's."

"How'd she do that?" Amy asked.

Mr. Ferguson had eagerly awaited the question. "She persuaded a friend to dress up like the queen. Then the countess arranged for Rohan to meet this impostor in the dead of night in the gardens of the palace of Versailles. It was too dark to see anything, so Rohan was thrilled when his queen, dressed all in white, presented him with a rose. She even allowed Rohan to kiss her slipper before she ran off into the darkness."

Mrs. Ferguson grinned. "Jamie's right, this sounds like a fairy tale. Are you making it up as you go along, dear?"

"It's history, Miriam; every word."

"Okay, who was the impostor?" she asked.

"*Another* shady lady named Nicole, a performer at the Palais-Royal . . . though some history books say she was the Baroness d'Olivia. Anyway, Rohan never suspected a thing because his friend Cagliostro had prophesied he'd meet a woman in white who would transform his life. Besides, Rohan had been completely blinded by his desire to gain the queen's favor."

"Why would she trick Rohan like that?" Jamie asked. "What was in it for the Countess de la What's-her-name?"

"Profit, naturally. Once Rohan was convinced Madame

de La Motte was a confidante of Her Majesty, she began borrowing money from him and said it was for the queen. It was common knowledge that the court of Louis the Sixteenth was deeply in debt, and had no ready cash."

"Oh, I get it," said Jamie. "Rohan figured he'd get in good with the queen by lending her money. Only he wasn't actually lending it to the queen, he was *giving* it to the shady lady."

"Exactly, Son. Rohan signed a paper agreeing to act as the queen's security. In reality, Rohan didn't have much cash himself, but he considered that a minor detail."

"Sounds like everyone was tricking everyone else," Amy commented.

"That's true," her father said, "but Rohan never imagined he'd have to make good the queen's debts. That's why he agreed to sign a note to cover the purchase of a priceless diamond necklace."

"Good," Amy said, "now we get to the necklace."

"And quite a necklace it was. It cost over four hundred thousand dollars and was made of the finest diamonds. Knowing of her passion for precious gems, Boehmer, the jeweler, had tried several times to sell it to Marie Antoinette. But each time she'd refused. Boehmer even threatened to commit suicide if she didn't buy it. When Madame de La Motte discovered this, she hatched her plan. Once she had Rohan's promissory note, *she* acquired the necklace, pretending it was for the queen."

"What a clever con artist," Mrs. Ferguson observed. "She wound up getting a priceless necklace for *nothing*."

"That's right," agreed Mr. Ferguson, "but things all began to fall apart when the first installment came due.

Boehmer contacted Rohan for payment and was told he'd have to wait. So naturally Boehmer went to Marie Antoinette to complain about the delay. That's when the deception was discovered. The queen accused Rohan of stealing the necklace, and Boehmer, realizing he'd been gypped, complained to the king."

"Haven't you left out something?" Amy asked. "What did Cagliostro have to do with all this?"

Mr. Ferguson smiled, pleased by the attentiveness of his captive audience. "Be patient, Amy, and allow history to unfold. Marie Antoinette was so furious, she ordered Boehmer arrested. Rohan was sent to the Bastille and Madame de La Motte was arrested too. To get herself off the hook, the countess blamed the entire mess on Cagliostro. At her trial she accused him of witchcraft and sorcery. She said he'd forced her into the whole affair."

"That's rotten," Jamie said, "but I don't see why it was such a big deal. After all, it was only a necklace. How could it cause the French Revolution?"

"Because history isn't created in a vacuum, Son. As I told you, there was lots of political unrest in France. To save the honor of the throne, Louis the Sixteenth ordered Parliament to try Rohan, and the whole thing became a public scandal. Accounts of everyone's testimony were published daily."

"Sort of like the nightly news?" Mrs. Ferguson asked.

"Even more sensational, Miriam. The trial lasted nine months. It became the most serious scandal in the country and the prologue to the Revolution. Even though the queen was blameless, her enemies insisted that she'd made Rohan her scapegoat. You see, everyone knew of

Marie Antoinette's extravagance and passion for diamonds. Countess de La Motte kept insisting Cagliostro had bewitched the queen. She said he was a false prophet, his séances were a swindle, and his cures worthless. Naturally, all this gossip was devoured daily by a fascinated public."

"Didn't Cagliostro defend himself?" Jamie asked.

"Well, he didn't help matters any by maintaining his innocence. He, too, was thrown into the Bastille, and all his wealth and property were confiscated."

"So he was put on trial too?" Amy asked.

"Yes, but he cut a ridiculous figure at his trial. He wore a gold embroidered coat and swaggered around like a ham actor. He concocted outlandish lies about his noble ancestry. The judge and spectators laughed at him, and no one believed a word he said after that. His reputation was in shreds, and he never recovered from the scandal."

"What happened to the shady lady who started it all?" Amy asked.

"And what happened to the necklace?" Mrs. Ferguson asked.

"The necklace mysteriously disappeared, Miriam. It was never seen again. As for Madame de La Motte, when she got out of prison she wrote a series of scandalous memoirs in which she accused Cagliostro all over again. She was always extravagant and constantly in debt. It was while attempting to escape one of her creditors that she climbed out a window and fell three floors. She died several weeks later. Poor Cagliostro spent a year in the Bastille, then was banished from France by the king. By then he was a penniless laughingstock, his reputation in ruins. Supposedly he died in 1795."

"Supposedly?" Amy asked. "What do you mean, Dad?"

"There's always been a mystery surrounding Cagliostro's death. After he fled to Rome, he eventually wound up in a prison at the hands of the Inquisition. He was thrown into a dungeon cut out of solid rock and was literally buried alive. While he was there, Cagliostro asked to confess to a priest. A priest, similar to him in size and appearance, arrived, and after a while he left. Some hours later a jailer entered the cell and found the body of a strangled man dressed in Cagliostro's clothes. But the priest himself was never seen again, and many people swore that the great magician was alive. Some people may think he's still alive today. You see, Cagliostro swore he was more than a thousand years old. He insisted his Elixir of Life maintained him. All he need do was regenerate himself every fifty years during a full moon in spring, in the company of one faithful person."

Jamie swallowed the last remaining gingersnap. "What a great story!"

"Are you sure you didn't make it up, Richard?"

"Not one word, Miriam. There you have it, folks—the infamous Affair of the Diamond Necklace."

Mrs. Ferguson cleared away the empty plates. "I guess you kids don't need to watch TV tonight—you've already had enough entertainment."

"Who needs TV?" Jamie asked excitedly. "Amy and I are going outside to discuss this some more."

Mr. Ferguson was delighted. "You kids want to discuss *history*?"

81

"Sure, Dad," Amy said. "That's the best history lesson I ever had!"

As the twins ran toward the porch, Mr. Ferguson glanced at his wife. "Miriam, are you sure you didn't put the kids up to this?"

"Why should I? You're in a fascinating field, Richard. The children finally realize that. Some people may have one adventure in their lifetime, but a historian is involved with adventures every day!"

Mr. Ferguson laughed. "Okay, honey, don't lay it on *too* thick; I think my depression has passed. Whatever the reason, it worked."

"That's good," said his wife, "maybe now you can put up those shelves in the pantry."

Mr. Ferguson smiled to himself. He glanced out the window and saw his children in heated discussion. Somehow, he could no longer mourn his misspent youth. In a burst of enthusiasm he dragged out his tool kit and eagerly began to work.

"I still say we have no proof," Jamie argued. "Okay, maybe Loogastric thinks he's Cagliostro; but that doesn't mean he is. Lots of wacky people think they're *Napoleon*."

"Then we'll get proof," Amy said with determination. "Right after the performance tonight."

Chapter Eleven

THE ACCIDENTS ON THE TWO PREVIOUS NIGHTS HAD HEIGHT-
ened the tension under the Fanzini big top. Although
Madame Fanzini commanded the crowd with her usual
forcefulness, there was anxiety in her voice as she introduced each act. She, like the audience, wondered the
same thing: Would something else go wrong?

The first half of the show proceeded smoothly. The
extra-added tension and excitement seemed to make the
performers excel even more. Julio and his lion act went
well, and Gino performed a three-high on the trampoline
which delighted the children in the stands.

The Barrel of Monkeys act produced its usual barrel of
laughter.

Maria and her rosinback horses were on next. As the
band began playing Strauss's "Thunder and Lightning
Polka," Maria came hurtling into the ring, circling the

sawdust like a whirlwind. She quickly threw a somersault, which took her over the back of a second horse to land on the back of a third as they cantered around the ring. The gleaming tiara on Maria's head made sparkling circles of showering light.

Then Lucio entered, doing his drunk act as he hung precariously from the horse's hindquarters. For a finale Lucio set three hoops on fire and Maria proceeded to jump through each.

As Maria reached the third hoop the circle of flame suddenly splayed out uncontrollably, creating a hazardous fireball. Fortunately, she landed on her horse's back before it veered to the side; now arching its neck, the animal raised its front legs and panicked. Within an instant all the other horses in the ring began a stampede to escape.

Everyone soon realized something had gone wrong. As propmen and handlers rushed into the ring to smother the flames, Lucio grabbed the lead horse's mane, jumped on his back, and corralled the others into position. The high-spirited animals gradually calmed down and proceeded toward the exit. Luckily, Lucio's quick thinking had saved the performers and audience from a thundering herd of horseflesh.

Amy stared at her brother in silence. She didn't need to say anything. They both realized three consecutive accidents defied the law of averages and meant far more than coincidence.

Madame Fanzini, obviously shaken, introduced the next act. At the end of the show she announced that the sideshow and midway attractions had been canceled until the following evening.

After the show the trailers surrounding the big top were deathly silent. True to the circus's tradition of privacy, the Fanzini Troupe had no desire to share their misfortunes with the "towners" of Monroe. They felt their troubles could be understood only by sympathetic circus folk who would be aware of both the risks taken nightly and the courage required to continue.

Amy knew this. But she was still surprised at the coolness of Madame Fanzini's tone when she spoke to her young visitors. "I can't talk to you now, children," she said sharply.

"Is Maria all right?" Jamie asked.

"She's fine," she replied, not wishing to elaborate.

"And the horses?" Amy asked. She was afraid one of them might have been injured during the stampede. "Did any get hurt in the fire?"

"No, we were lucky."

To Jamie, that was an ironic statement, considering all the bad luck they'd been having.

"Excuse me," said Madame Fanzini, and entered her trailer, "I can't talk anymore." She closed the door behind her.

"I think she senses something too," Amy said as they walked away. "She knows all these things aren't accidents."

"Then why doesn't she call the police?" Jamie asked.

"Circus people are too proud for that, Jamie. Gino said they always keep their problems to themselves."

An occasional flashlight beam cut through the darkness

CHESTER PUBLIC LIBRARY
CHESTER, ILLINOIS

of the midway as some performers hurried toward their trailers. Amy hurried, too, hoping to catch up with one of them. She noticed the clown they had seen the night before; his face still wore its painted-on grin.

"You two snooping around again?" he asked sharply. "Scram, you've no business here."

"We're not doing anything wrong," Jamie argued.

"You'd better not," the clown threatened. Taking a beer can from his baggy pants, he gulped down its contents. "This mud show is jinxed enough already. I'll probably blow this troupe any day now." The surly clown threw the can into the trash, then shuffled away.

"There's something awfully suspicious about that guy," said Jamie. "I think we should follow him and see what he's up to."

Amy wasn't listening. She was receiving a premonition of more immediate danger. In her mind's eye she could see the broken, trampled body of one of the Fanzinis lying bloodied on the ground! There would be more danger that night!

Suddenly Amy heard the frenzied trumpeting of the elephants. Her horrid vision was about to become a reality.

"Hurry, Jamie," she shouted, and ran toward the animal wagons. "Something awful is about to happen!"

Jamie followed quickly behind. As they reached the wagons, Amy screamed out, "Be careful!" just as Gino was helping Rick herd the elephants into their cages.

For some reason a large bull at the front frantically resisted entering the cage. He lifted his trunk, threw up his front feet, and trumpeted wildly. Amy knew that in another second the elephant's huge legs would crash to the ground, crushing Gino beneath them. She rushed toward the boy, pulled him aside, and they both fell to the ground. As the elephant's legs struck the dirt, Amy and Gino crawled to safety.

Sensing something was wrong, the other elephants in line began jostling out of position, screeching in frenzy. It took several minutes for their handler to calm them down by slapping them soundly on their backs.

Gino got up from the ground, brushing the dirt from his jeans. "Thanks," he said, still out of breath, "I'm lucky you guys were around."

Jamie helped his sister up, then asked, "What got into those animals? It looked like they were going crazy."

"I don't know," Gino confessed. "The elephants never give us any trouble; they're sweet as babies."

After the animals had returned to normal, Rick went into their cage. He discovered several damp rags positioned in each corner. "This is what got them bulls all stirred up," he said. He held out the rags for the children to see.

Gino sniffed them. "Alcohol! No wonder they went nuts. Elephants *hate* alcohol. The smell of it drives them insane."

"Who could've stuck those rags in there?" Amy asked.

"Beats me, girlie," Rick said. "Maybe someone was mopping up a mess and threw them aside. But we all had a mighty close call just now. Those bulls are gentle giants; but they can still crush a human skull! We're sure glad you passed by when you did."

"We sure are," Gino agreed. "It's almost as if you knew something was—"

Before Gino could finish his thought, the circus vet came running from the horse tent.

"What's up, Harris?" asked Rick.

"We have to ditch that last bale of hay," the vet explained. "Two of the rosinbacks are down; I've just given them injections."

"Ditch it, but why? I checked it myself. That hay was number-one timothy—the very best."

"It's moldy," said the vet. "I only hope those geldings don't get *botulism*. I hope I got to them in time."

Rick threw up his hands in disgust. "This has been some season so far. What next? I wonder."

No one had long to wait to find out. Salome, the snake charmer, hurried from her trailer, obviously upset. Baby, her twenty-foot Indian rock python was missing.

"What do you mean, it's missing?" asked Rick.

"Just what I said. She always sleeps in the cage beside my bed, but she's gone. Poor Baby was so upset when the sideshow was canceled tonight. She loves to meet people."

"We can't have that snake wandering around near the wagons," Rick said with concern.

"I know that," Salome said, equally concerned. "Someone might *frighten* her."

Suddenly insane screeching began to come from the monkey cages, and everyone ran to see what had caused it.

All the monkeys were hanging from their bars screaming in terror as Baby coiled her way along the side of the cage, hissing menacingly.

"Quick, get Claudio," Rick said.

88

Gino hurried off toward the trainer's trailer.

Salome gently stroked her python to calm it down. She cooed and whispered baby talk until the huge snake uncoiled itself from the bars and draped itself around Salome's neck.

Claudio, throwing on his robe, came rushing from his trailer. "What's wrong with my monkeys?" he asked. Seeing the snake, he quickly realized what had happened. "No wonder they're upset. Monkeys can't stand the hiss of a snake. You know that, Salome," he said accusingly. "Keep that thing locked up or I'll turn it into a pair of shoes!"

Salome, distressed at the mere thought of having her beloved Baby turned into footwear, began to cry. "I didn't let Baby out," she said. "Someone broke the lock on her cage!"

"Come off it, Salome," Claudio said. "Who'd do a thing like that?"

"That's what I'd like to know," she said, wiping away her tears. "Just make sure your monkeys don't frighten her again!" With the python draped around her like a collar, Salome raised her head haughtily and walked back to her trailer.

Hoping to placate his monkeys with a snack, Claudio grabbed an orange from the fruit bucket. He peeled it and handed each of them a piece. There were several more minutes of screeching, and then they finally settled down.

"Snakes are the one thing these creatures can't stand," Claudio explained. "Monkeys don't mind the noise of

89

kids screaming at them all day, but if they hear a snake hiss, they go crazy."

As Amy listened to Claudio, she realized whoever was causing the accidents knew each animal's weak point!

Amy sensed that Gino was thinking the same thing. "I'd better go now," said Gino. "Thanks for—well, for being around."

Gino waved good-bye and walked away. Amy knew the boy now realized the hard luck his family had been having might actually be sabotage, but he did not know who was causing it. Amy, however, was certain she knew. "Well, Jamie, are you finally convinced something awful is going on here?"

"Sure, that's obvious and I've my own ideas who's to blame. Why do you keep insisting it's Loogastric? You have no proof he's involved."

"We came here for proof," she reminded him.

As the twins rounded the side of the animal wagons, they saw Loogastric's trailer in the distance, still set apart from all the others. The drapes were now open, and the flickering light of a candle burned in the window. To their surprise, the door was open as well. They tiptoed closer. The trailer seemed empty.

"Where do you suppose he went?" asked Amy.

"Maybe he's in the cookhouse having coffee," Jamie suggested. "Or maybe he's out back somewhere," he added teasingly, "mixing up a new batch of that Elixir of Life."

"Remember what Jeb said," Amy cautioned. "Don't laugh at things you don't understand."

"Who's laughing? This whole deal has given me the

creeps. We don't know which wild beast will go nuts next; this place isn't safe."

"Shh," Amy said, and peeked in through the trailer door. She noticed a large crystal ball resting on a table.

Jamie grabbed her arm. "You're not going inside, are you?"

"I have to," Amy said, suddenly drawn toward the crystal. The clear transparent sphere radiated all the colors of the spectrum, and an aura encircled it. Amy felt powerless to resist the hypnotic pull of its energy. She clasped Jamie's hand. He, too, felt himself being drawn near the crystal, as if magnetized.

The children stood motionless, gazing into its depths as scenes bathed in iridescent colors unfolded before their eyes. They saw figures in landscapes of an unknown past.

Thought, emotion, space, and time far beyond physical consciousness all seemed encapsulated within the magical sphere. A chain of human experience comprising the history of earth played out its drama, one century following the other, yet each lasted no more than seconds in time.

To the children, it seemed they were watching a film played at a fantastically rapid speed. Each image barely registered visually, yet some other aspect of their being had recorded it.

Through this maze of collective memory one person kept reappearing in every scene that unfolded. It was Loogastric.

In the first image the Great Pyramid of Khufu at Gizeh rose in the background, majestic and eloquent. Loogastric stood before it, draped in gold robes. He raised his jeweled wand, and a luminous haze entered the atmosphere, until the air was a mass of shining particles. Loogastric was the master of light, the keeper of the secret luminance of the Mysteries. He was the chosen one, friend of Isis and Osiris, more powerful than the pharaoh.

The vision vanished, and another image appeared. In it the Parthenon of Athens rose at the center of a landscape of vast ancient temples. With flaming torches by his side, Loogastric was performing the secret rites of Eleusis.

The vision changed again.

Here now Druid priests were imparting their doctrines in the depths of forests and the darkness of caves. As they emerged to complete their rituals beneath the sacred rocks of Stonehenge, it was Loogastric who led the ceremony.

Images moved even more quickly now.

The Colosseum in Rome and the gladiators of the Circus Maximus.

Knights in gleaming armor swiftly flashed before their eyes. The Crusades and the age of chivalry. Still, Loogastric was the most powerful magus in the land, with more followers than Merlin.

Yes, Loogastric was ever-present. He was the premier magician and adept, in control of the Forces.

Now came the grandiose palaces of kings, the splendor of Versailles, the opulence of Marie Antoinette's court, and there, too, stood Loogastric. Throughout recorded time the Grand Copt had been present, immortal and supreme.

For an instant the vision within the crystal clouded.

Then an image far more recent emerged. It was the big top, its huge canvas resting in the field like a silent sentinel beneath the light of the full moon. Loogastric stood beside it, with a comically insignificant companion at his side. As Loogastric waved his wand the number 5,557 appeared above his head. This was evidence that another cycle of eternity would soon commence. Once again the universe would become the tool of the magician.

Again the quicksilver image changed. Now the twins viewed *themselves* as they stared into the crystal. And the image kept repeating itself in the crystal's fathomless depths. They stared at the dizzying vision of gradually diminishing images as if it were a whirlpool sucking them into its depths—drawing them toward darkness and oblivion.

Then the images ceased.

A light was switched on inside the trailer, and Loogastric stood in the doorway. He wore a long black robe, and his head was draped in a turban of gold. Scarabs and symbols hung from his neck, and a sword was suspended from his silken belt.

He spoke in a voice filled with vengeful arrogance. "What you have seen within the crystal is Truth. I am the noble traveler through time, possessor of the Mystery of Mysteries: the arcanum arcanorum. Behold me and be fearful, for I can harness the Powers of the Ages."

Jamie did not think so. He was not sure what they had seen in the crystal, but it certainly wasn't Truth. More likely, it was a hypnotic spell which the magician had put them under—an illusion far removed from reality.

But Amy sensed Loogastric's awesome powers and

had no wish to incur his wrath. Yet she could not help asking "Why are you doing these awful things?"

The magician's voice roared in exultation. "Within the formulas of Magick all acts must be equal. Do not persist in questioning my actions. Revenge may be bitter fruit, but it is my just harvest."

"Why do you want revenge?" Amy asked. "What for?"

In the flickering candlelight, shadows seemed to creep from every corner. Raising himself to his full height, Loogastric towered before them. "Now is not the only time," he explained with a dark, disapproving scowl. "Now is nothing but a time for retribution. My mortal form has suffered much humiliation. Though I possess all powers, I am forbidden their use." He drew closer to Amy, his dark eyes blazing. "Hear me now, initiate, my circle has been rendered impregnable. Do not thwart those powers which are permitted me, lest I be tempted to defy the Universal Force. Do not incur the wrath of my Brotherhood, lest I produce a mass of maggots which will swarm over the carrion earth to execute my pleasure among the legions of the living. Begone from this place and speak not a word of what you have seen."

Jamie couldn't wait to be gone. He was halfway out the door when Loogastric hurried over to block his exit. "Do not forget," he cautioned, "the Powers of the Ages have decreed that what shall be here shall be so. My memory is long, and crimes committed against me must be revenged."

"Sure, I'll remember," Jamie said. He was in such a hurry to leave, he nearly fell down the steps of the trailer. As Amy followed, Loogastric slammed the metal door behind them.

Jamie breathed a sigh of relief. "I was wrong about that guy; he's not a wacko, he's a *super*wacko. He's a candidate for a straitjacket!"

Amy didn't agree. "Don't dismiss his powers, Jamie. What about those things we saw in the crystal?"

"They were all *tricks*, Amy. After all, illusion is the guy's business. Which proves my point about his being a nut. With great tricks like that, he could be making a fortune instead of traveling around with a one-ring circus."

As the twins walked back toward the circus wagons, Amy realized there was still an unexplained element to the mystery. But she knew one thing: Loogastric was indeed the infamous Cagliostro, the possessor of great power. Now not only were the Fanzinis in danger, but she and Jamie were too.

As the twins circled around the elephant cages, two hands reached out through the darkness and grabbed them by the wrists. They both screamed and made a frantic effort to escape.

They heard a voice whisper from inside the cage. "Shhh, keep it down, will you. I've just gotten these bulls quiet, don't set 'em off again." It was Rick, the handler; he was seated on the ground. "Didn't mean to startle you kids, but I wasn't sure who you were."

"You nearly scared us to death," Jamie said. "What're you doing in there?"

"Trying to get some sleep," he explained.

"In the elephant cage?" Amy asked. "Why?"

"Trainers always sleep with their bulls when they get

antsy; it's tradition. It calms 'em down and makes 'em feel confident. Besides," he added, "I'm also keeping an eye on the circus grounds. Something strange is going on, in case you haven't noticed."

"Oh, we noticed!" said Jamie.

Rick yawned, slapped one of the elephant's feet, then smoothed down his sleeping bag. "You kids better get home now," he said. "And watch your step on the way."

Chapter Twelve

"DON'T TAKE THIS PERSONALLY," JAMIE SAID THE NEXT DAY, "but I think you and Jeb are all wet."

The twins were seated in the Sweet Shoppe, where Jamie had just ordered his second monster mash sundae, complete with three scoops of Rocky Road, butterscotch syrup, chopped walnuts, chocolate chips, and raspberry swirl whipped cream.

Amy sipped her pineapple soda, marveling at her brother's ability to consume so many calories. "How can you have an appetite after what happened last night? I barely slept a wink."

"Brain food," he explained.

Emma Bradbury, whose husband owned the Sweet Shoppe, approached their booth and plunked down Jamie's second helping. "Everything okay, kids?"

"Just great, Mrs. Bradbury," Jamie said, and dug in.

"That's what I like"—she smiled—"a boy with an appetite. I had Henry throw a few extra cherries on this one—for my best customer." She patted Jamie's head, then returned to the counter.

"You should try one of these, Amy," he said, wiping whipped cream from his mouth. "If your brain worked properly, you wouldn't get so many goofy ideas."

Amy found her brother's know-it-all attitude as infuriating as ever. "Okay, tell me what *you* think happened last night."

"Like I said, Loogastric is a great illusionist. I'm not sure how he produced all those images in his crystal ball, but I'll bet there's a simple scientific principle behind it. He probably hypnotized us."

"You're the one who's all wet, Jamie. Loogastric is Cagliostro. He caused all those accidents."

"Think *logically*," Jamie insisted. "Listen. For the sake of argument, let's say I agree with you. If Loogastric really had supernatural powers, he could harness a lightning bolt and zap the circus up in smoke, right? He wouldn't need to sneak around cutting cable wires, throwing rags at elephants, and sticking a snake in the monkey cage."

Amy had to agree. "That's what I don't understand. Loogastric doesn't seem to be *using* his magical powers. But he has them, Jamie, I know it. He admitted he wanted revenge."

"For what? Why would anyone want to harm the Fanzinis? They're all real nice people."

"I know it doesn't make sense, but Jebediah said—"

"Listen, I'm sure Jeb's a swell guy, but maybe he's not as smart as you think. He's just a ghost, not a genius."

"You wouldn't say that to his face," Amy said, defending her ancestor.

"I've never *seen* his face! But if he were sitting with us right now, I'd say the same thing."

A gust of fresh spring air flowed through the Sweet Shoppe as several children ran through the open door and hurried toward the counter. After they were seated, Amy noticed that the cool air seemed to remain. It hung suspended above the booth like a palpable presence. Jamie felt it too. He shivered, then pushed his bowl aside. "This ice cream is giving me the chills."

Amy did not hear her brother. She was staring at the seat beside her. A vaporous form had begun to appear. Its smoky wisps combined within the air until they had taken on the shape of Jebediah Aloysious Tredwell. He was seated next to Amy, his military uniform as immaculate as always, its brass buttons shining.

"Jeb," she gasped, "what are you doing *here?*"

"Defending my honor, Cousin, against all those who seek to profane it." Jebediah's spirit stared at Jamie from across the booth. "Hear me, lad, and take heed. I do not make my intermittent and all-too-brief appearances in order to communicate *fabrications*. If anyone, be he man or boy, has cause to doubt my veracity, let him say as much to my face!"

Jamie looked in the direction of Amy's stare but saw only the blank wall of the booth. "Is Jeb really here?" he whispered. "And did he just call me an *ass?*"

"Sort of; I think he's angry."

"Well, what's he doing here?" Jamie asked nervously. "Why'd you summon him?"

"I didn't; he just *came*."

Jamie was taken aback. "Jeb's ghost can't materialize here. This is the Sweet Shoppe."

Jebediah had no such doubts regarding where his spirit might choose to appear. In fact, he seemed singularly pleased with his surroundings. He glanced around at the display cases filled with slices of pie and cake and at the colorful posters illustrating banana splits, chocolate malts, and giant sundaes. "This is truly a marvelous confectionery," he observed. "Mr. Bradbury runs a most delightful establishment." He leaned over to examine the half-eaten sundae in Jamie's bowl; the ice cream was beginning to melt under its topping of nuts, chocolate chips, syrup, and raspberry swirl. "What do you call such a concoction as this?" he asked.

"Monster mash," Amy said.

"Indeed? It seems a most monstrous creation—quite unlike the parfaits I was pleased to partake of at Dolley Madison's table." The lieutenant colonel sniffed Amy's drink. "And this, Cousin?" he asked.

"It's called pineapple soda," said Amy.

"Amazing," said Jebediah, obviously impressed. "Tell me, Cousin, do you think the proprietor of this establishment knows how to concoct a capillaire?"

"What's that?" she asked.

"A simple libation flavored with orange-flower water, almonds, and syrup of maidenhair fern."

Mrs. Bradbury passed by the booth and asked, "Anything else I can get you kids?"

"I don't think so," Amy said, "unless you happen to have some capillaire."

"Cap of what, honey?"

"Never mind."

Mrs. Bradbury nodded, then walked away.

Jebediah sighed wistfully. "Perhaps 'tis just as well, Cousin. In my later years my diet was restricted to flummery. Youth's overindulgences invariably gave me the collywobbles."

Jamie leaned over and whispered in Amy's ear. "I can't understand a word. It sounded like Jeb said *collywobbles*."

"Enough of reverie," Jeb said sternly. "We must get to the point at hand. I have materialized because I sense your distress. Have you not taken my words of warning?"

"*I* have," Amy said. "We figured out what you were trying to tell us, Jeb. I know Loogastric is really Cagliostro, the evil magician. But Jamie doesn't agree. He says the accidents at the circus weren't caused by black magic."

"That's right," Jamie said, firm in his opinion. "Someone else is messing things up over there, I'm sure of it."

"Perhaps you are *both* right," Jebediah said. "To grasp Truth as a whole, one must grasp its individual parts. Intrigue may very well be fermenting within the circus encampment. Conversely, Cagliostro may have awesome powers yet not be at liberty to use them."

"That's what he told us," Amy said, "but I didn't understand what he meant. If he has supernatural powers, why wouldn't he use them?"

"Child, first you must understand the Universal Law. A supreme magus must always be cautious in the use of his powers, for he cannot dictate their policy. He must always act in accord with the properties of his position at that time within time. To do otherwise would be to break the keys of Magick and to render havoc unto himself. Even one possessing great power must conform to the Universal Rules. He cannot sever the bonds which unite all things within the whole, lest he release the Dark Night of his own soul."

By this time Jamie had begun to tune in to what Jeb was saying. "I get it; it's sort of like the Golden Rule in reverse. If Loogastric goes around zapping people with his power, he'll get zapped himself."

"Indeed so, James. Your phrase is apt, albeit in modern parlance."

"But I still don't buy this whole idea of magic," he argued.

Jeb's spirit seemed incredulous. "The unseen exists, call it what you will. Surely my presence proves that much. Mark me, Cousin, do not dismiss that which you cannot comprehend. Realize that a word for Magick is found within every language in every era of recorded time; in every society, such human symbolism has emerged. Shadows only, perhaps; but shadows cast by something *real*."

"No, it doesn't make sense," Jamie insisted. "We've met lots of the Fanzini family and they're all terrific people. Why would Loogastric want to hurt them?"

"That's right, Jeb," Amy said. "Loogastric said he wanted revenge, but we don't know why. Why should he want to kill the Fanzinis and destroy their circus?"

"If one seeks an answer in the wrong place, one finds nothing," Jeb explained.

"You mean the answer isn't at the circus?" Amy said.

"I mean the answer may not be within this time. The wheel of time has many spokes, just as the Tree of Life has many branches. As with my apple trees, the blossoms fall yet the roots remain."

At that moment the children were distracted as Mrs. Bradbury shouted across the shop to her husband behind the counter. "Henry, what's holding up my two orders of pecan pie with double scoops of maple walnut?"

"Hold your horses, Em," Mr. Bradbury shouted back.

As Amy turned to resume the conversation with Jebediah she saw that he had disappeared.

Jamie, unaware that the ghost had vanished, continued. "I didn't understand what you said, Jeb. What do apple trees have to do with this deal?"

"Forget it," said Amy, "Jeb's gone."

"Gone?" he grumbled. "That guy is no help at all! C'mon, Amy, let's get over to the library."

"What for?"

"We have to find the answer somewhere, so let's read up on magic!"

"Here it is," said Jamie, leafing through a very old, very heavy book called *Precepts of Magic*. "This explains those numbers 5,557 we saw in Loogastric's crystal ball. According to this, a magician can regenerate himself for 5,557 years."

"How?"

"Just like Dad told us. Every fifty years he has to retreat into the country with one faithful friend in the month of May during a full moon. If he drinks only May dew and eats only new and tender herbs, on the fortieth day he'll have his youth and health again."

"I guess that's what Cagliostro has been doing for centuries."

"Maybe," said Jamie, "but that diet sounds deadly. Besides, a goofy guy like Loogastric might have a hard time finding one faithful friend. Everyone in the eighteenth century wound up thinking he was a screwball!"

"I wonder why Cagliostro didn't use his magic powers then, to get himself released from prison."

"Maybe this is why," said Jamie, reading aloud. " 'Ceremonial magic is an ancient art whereby a magician may control the invisible inhabitants of the astral world, and is not necessarily evil. But black magic involves the damnation of the magician's soul.' "

"Then it's just like Jeb told us," Amy said.

The word *time* kept running through Amy's head as she recalled the words the magician had used: *"Now is not the only time."* Jeb himself had told them the same thing. "Maybe the clue to all this lies in another time, Jamie."

Jamie was pondering the word *time* as well. He remembered what their father had told them: "History isn't created in a vacuum." At the time that Cagliostro was involved in Marie Antoinette's scandal, lots of other things were happening too.

"You're right, Amy," he agreed, "that may be our big clue. Signore Fanzini told us his ancestor Cesare performed for Marie Antoinette. There's got to be a connection."

"Do you think Cagliostro wants revenge for something Cesare Fanzini did?"

"Possibly, but what could it be? After all, Cesare was only a performer in the queen's court."

"I don't know." Amy sighed. "The answer is probably staring us right in the face and we can't see it."

Jamie, still deep in thought, suddenly received a revelation. All the confusing pieces of the puzzle were now falling together to form a clear picture. "That's it," he shouted excitedly. "The answer *has* been staring us in the face—every single night. C'mon, Amy, we've got to get over to the circus grounds right away!"

Chapter Thirteen

DUSK HAD ALREADY BEGUN TO FALL WHEN THE TWINS HURRIED from the library and headed for the Monroe football field.

Jamie checked his watch. "Faster, Amy, the show starts in about an hour. If we don't get there before the performance, there may be another accident."

Amy was aware of the imminent danger, but she still had no idea what her brother had discovered. "I can't run any faster," she complained, pausing to catch her breath. "Please tell me what's going on. Have you figured out why Cagliostro wants revenge?"

"Sure, haven't you? It's the diamond necklace, Amy; that's what he's after."

"The necklace? You mean Marie Antoinette's jewels?"

"Naturally. Don't you get it? If Cagliostro could've produced those jewels at his trial, he might've proved that Madame What's-her-face had been to blame for the whole mess. But the necklace disappeared, remember? It was never seen again. The way I figure it, the jewels were probably so hot, they were smuggled out of the country. Madame What's-her-name ditched the evidence as fast as she could. She probably thought she could get the diamonds back again after her trial was over; only she died before she could track them down."

"But where are they?" Amy asked. "Who took them?"

"Nobody took them; they were *given away*. I'll bet that crooked countess gave them to Cesare Fanzini as a gift for his performance. Cesare had that special seal allowing him to travel out of the country, remember? I'm sure he never knew the jewels were real."

Amy still did not get it. "No, Dad said everyone in France knew about that diamond necklace. Whoever that shady lady gave it to would've suspected something."

"Not if it wasn't a necklace any longer," Jamie explained. "Jewel thieves smuggled their loot by *changing the settings*. That's what the countess did. She turned the necklace into something else so no one would suspect."

As evening settled in, the lampposts in Monroe switched on and the twins could see the big top light up in the distance.

As they picked up their pace, Amy pondered her brother's theory. It seemed credible. Yes, it was possible the infamous diamonds still existed. It was even possible the person who had them did not realize their actual value. But she still didn't know who had them.

"Okay, I give up," she said, "where are the diamonds now?"

It was painfully evident that Jamie did not plan to

come right out with the answer. His ingenious deductions had brought him to this point of discovery, and he chose to savor the moment. "It's just like you said, Amy; they've been staring us in the face all the time."

Amy found her brother's smugness maddening. "They have?"

"Yep. We've seen them every night at the circus."

"We have?" As Amy thought back, an image of Maria Fanzini flashed in her mind. She saw Maria astride her horse, her gleaming tiara sparkling on her head. Then she thought back to their first meeting with the Fanzinis, when Maria had asked to wear the headpiece during rehearsal. She remembered that Madame Fanzini kept it locked in a strongbox and that, by tradition, it was only worn during performances. "You mean the *tiara?*" Amy said. "You think that's what Cagliostro wants?"

"I'll bet you a monster mash sundae!"

"Then why doesn't he take it?"

"Listen, I don't pretend to understand all this black magic mumbo jumbo," Jamie said, "but according to Jeb, Cagliostro can't use supernatural powers to get what he wants. If he does, his soul will be damned and he won't be able to regenerate himself again. So he can only use his *human* skills to get that necklace, and the only skills he has as a magician are illusion and hypnotism."

"But what about all those accidents?" Amy asked.

"Cagliostro must have an accomplice inside the circus," Jamie reasoned. "Someone else is doing all the dirty work for him."

Amy thought back to the vision of the big top that they had seen within the crystal. Yes, Cagliostro had a companion in the image—someone who seemed very familiar. Amy tried to grasp the vision more clearly, but Jamie continued to hurry her along.

As they approached the circus grounds they could hear the band tuning up beneath the canvas. The old sailmaker was stitching up another tear in the seams of the canvas and several of the trainers were giving the animals a run-through before the performance.

"We have to get to the Fanzinis' trailer," said Jamie. "We need to warn them that the tiara will probably be stolen."

As the twins hurried toward the trailer camp, they heard the strains of an operatic aria coming from the phonograph in the Fanzini trailer. Drawing closer, they noticed that all the lights were on and the door was open. They glanced in but saw no one inside. Clothing was scattered around in an untypically untidy fashion. The children realized the Fanzinis must have left in great haste, which signified trouble somewhere.

"Where do you suppose they went?" Jamie asked.

"I don't know," said Amy, growing uneasy, "but something's wrong." She was receiving another psychic premonition. "We have to find Maria; she's in danger."

"Another accident?" Jamie said. "But the show hasn't started yet."

"No, she's not in the ring," Amy said, "she's in her trailer."

The children raced frantically down the row of trailers parked beside the big top, in search of Maria's.

"That must be it," said Jamie, pointing to one with a rosinback painted along its side.

Closer now, they could see Maria's figure through the window. She was wearing her pink sequined costume and held the jeweled tiara in her outstretched hands. The diamonds set in its crown glittered like stars as they caught the gleam from the lamplight.

The twins tiptoed to the door. Maria, they saw, was not alone. Loogastric was also inside the trailer. Draped in his velvet robes, he wore a conical hat and held a pentacle in one hand. He poured a circle of salt around the area in which he stood.

Maria stood motionless, watching him.

When Loogastric had finished, he raised his wand and spoke. "Ammon, Ra, and Osiris, hear my sacred invocation. I am the Magus Sorcerer who walks alone through time. I have seen beyond the Vale of Mysteries into the hidden caves and dark places. I shall keep my bond, lest I be sucked down into their turbid depths."

The twins stood silently in the doorway, uncertain what to do.

"I think he's putting a spell on Maria," whispered Amy.

"Maybe he's hypnotizing her."

"Well, shouldn't we try to stop him?"

"I don't know," said Jamie, "if she's already in a trance, that might be dangerous. Anyway, I've heard a hypnotist can't make a person do anything against their will."

Loogastric pointed the wand in Maria's direction, then began to chant:

"No super forces must I use,
No astral knowledge thus abuse.

Let only justice come to me.
As I will, so mote it be."

Slowly Maria began walking toward the magician. Her eyes were glazed; she had been hypnotized. "What do you want?" she asked.

"Justice," Loogastric replied. "Are you not aware of the dangers which have befallen your family?"

"I am," she answered in a monotone. "Everyone is afraid."

"I have it within my power to relieve that fear," he explained. "That which you hold in your hand has caused many disasters. Relinquish it willingly and your ill luck shall cease."

Maria stared into Loogastric's eyes. She held out the tiara, offering it to him. But then she quickly pulled it back. "No, I can't let you have it," she said. "It belonged to my ancestor Cesare. It has always been in the family; I can't give it up."

"You *must*," Loogastric said. "At this moment the black beast is poised to strike at your kinsman's throat. His blood shall run, and each drop shall be upon your hands!"

The twins, still standing in the doorway, felt the hypnotic power of the magician's words.

Once again Maria held out the tiara toward Loogastric. "Then take it," she said.

"Do you give it unto me willingly?" he asked.

"I do," she replied.

Loogastric quickly grasped the tiara and held it up in the air. "Oh, hear my custodians of the Secret Truths," he roared in exultation. "My long journey has at last been rewarded. I, the Great Copt, am that I am. In the time beyond time I shall be vindicated!"

The hypnotic spell seemed broken. Maria blinked and turned around just as Loogastric hurried through the doorway.

Amy, too, had been thrust back into reality, and now she stared into Loogastric's cold unyielding eyes as he stood before her. For a brief moment she was tempted to lunge toward him and grab the tiara but was stopped by the horrid vision that flashed warningly through her mind: Julio was being mauled to death by a black panther!

"Hear me, initiate," said Loogastric, "if you attempt to thwart me in this action, you shall take the consequences."

Both Amy and Jamie backed away. The magician thrust the tiara into the pocket of his robe and hurried down the midway, just as Maria came running down the steps of her trailer.

"What happened?" she asked.

"The Great Loogastric took off with your tiara," Jamie explained.

"Yes, now I remember; I gave it to him. I had a terrible feeling something awful would happen to Julio if I didn't."

Suddenly the frightening roar of a big cat filled the air, followed by a bloodcurdling scream. "Julio!" Maria shouted. "Something's wrong!"

She and the twins ran across the grounds until they reached the lion cages. There, Signore Fanzini was standing supported by a cane while his wife stood beside him. She held her hands to her mouth, trying to stifle another scream. Her son Julio was inside the training cage. He was trying to subdue the new black panther, which stood poised at his throat, ready to strike.

The huge cat lunged at Julio, knocking him down and ripping away at his arm. Just then one of the lions leapt over his fallen body. The panther quickly turned and began to engage in fierce combat with the lion, allowing Julio to crawl to the safety of a corner. Blood spilling from his arm, Julio managed to exit the cage while the two wild animals were still mauling each other.

Within minutes two more trainers came by to help. They lassoed the two big cats by the waist, pulling them off each other.

Madame Fanzini, still distraught, grabbed her son to her. "My God, are you badly hurt?"

"It's nothing, Mama, just scratches." Julio ripped the sleeve from his shirt and wrapped it around his injured arm.

"That new cat is no good, Son," said Signore Fanzini. "He must've been bottle-fed."

"No, Papa, he's a jungle cat. He's been good all through his first month of training. I don't understand what upset him."

Madame Fanzini neared the cage. "I do," she said, staring inside. The young panther was now subdued, lying on the ground, panting. Across his side could be seen the bloodied marks of two whiplashes. "Who has soiled the honor of the Fanzinis?" she asked, anger in her voice. "We *never* beat an animal into submission. Put fear in the heart of an animal and you make him a *killer!*"

Julio, fearing his mother's wrath far more than his

wounds, protested. "I'd never do that, Mama; you know that. I make the cats my friends, not my enemies."

Just then Rick and Gino came running toward the cages. Rick was dragging a man by the arm; the man himself was making vain attempts to resist. As they drew closer Amy recognized him. It was the surly clown who had spoken to them on two previous occasions. He was wearing his costume and the artificial grin.

"Signore Fanzini," Rick shouted, "the mystery is solved." He pushed the clown in front of him. "Barney here is the one responsible for everything."

"You've got no proof," Barney shouted. As he tried to run away, Rick shoved him up against the cage.

"Oh, yes, we have," said Gino, holding up a whip. "Here it is." There was a patch of dried blood on the tip, clear evidence that the panther had been beaten. "We found this in Barney's costume," explained Gino. "And we found the broken lock from Salome's python cage in his trailer. *He's* the one who's been causing all the accidents."

"That's right," said Rick. "Me and Gino suspected someone was sabotaging things, so we've been keeping our eyes open. Barney has bottles of booze stashed in his trailer too. He's the one who threw those alcohol rags into my elephant cage."

"That ain't proof," Barney protested. "Someone could've planted that stuff on me."

Signore Fanzini, a just man, needed to be certain. "Are you sure of this, Rick? What you've told me is a serious thing."

"You bet I'm sure," said Rick. He slammed Barney up

against the cage again, then thrust his arm underneath the clown's throat. "Shall we prove it, Barney? I'll just waltz you over to my elephant cage and let my bulls have a look at you, okay? Those stories you hear about an elephant's memory aren't just stories, Barney. Yeah, they're real smart, they are. They can remember a person's face for years. They know who threw those rags inside their cage, and if they ever see that guy come near them again, they'll *remember him!*"

The thought of being trampled to death by a herd of revenging elephants gave Barney pause. "Okay," he said, "I confess; but the whole deal wasn't my idea."

"Then whose was it?" asked Rick.

"I can tell you that," Jamie said. "It was the Great Loogastric. He wanted to frighten everybody in the circus."

"That magician?" asked Signore Fanzini. "Why? What do you children know about all this?"

As the Fanzinis stared at the twins, Amy was tempted to reveal the entire situation; but she knew they would find most of it impossible to believe. "He wanted the tiara," she explained. "Loogastric couldn't hypnotize Maria into giving it to him unless she thought her family's lives were in danger."

"That's right," Jamie continued. "Loogastric planned the whole thing just so he could make Maria give him the tiara."

"It's true, Papa," said Maria. "When Loogastric came into my trailer, I felt I had to give up the tiara or else more terrible things would happen to Fanzinis."

"This is all ridiculous," said Madame Fanzini. "Who

115

would cause such injury to get hold of a few pieces of sparkling glass? It makes no sense."

"That tiara isn't glass," Jamie said. "Your ancestor Cesare may have owned very valuable jewels."

"Valuable?" Signore Fanzini asked. "Yes, to our family they were very valuable. They represent two hundred years of circus history. But they have no value to anyone else."

"Loogastric seemed to think so," Jamie said.

"Then we must confront him and get at the truth," Armando Fanzini said firmly.

In a group, they all marched across the circus grounds toward the Great Loogastric's trailer. But the spot where the trailer had been parked was now empty.

Barney laughed. "I knew he'd be gone by now."

"Is what these children say true?" Lorenza Fanzini asked. "Were you the accomplice for this magician's crimes?"

Clenching his teeth, Barney spit out his words. "I ain't saying nothin' else. Call the cops if ya like. A jail cell is a darn sight better than being in an elephant cage."

"We'll have no police here," Signore Fanzini said. "The circus solves its own problems; that is tradition. I want you off these grounds right away, Barney. You're *finished* with this troupe."

Barney leered beneath his painted grin. "Who cares? I've got other fish to fry. I'll be outta here in no time; watch my dust!" The clown hurried down the field, away from the big top.

"Signore, why are you letting him get away?" Rick asked.

116

Armando Fanzini sighed. "I think it's best; we have no real proof of anything. Besides, those who do wrong never get away. They drag their sins wherever they go, and sooner or later they must pay for them."

"But the *tiara*, Grandpa," Maria said sadly. "It's *my* fault it's gone."

Madame Fanzini hugged her granddaughter. "Why should we care for *things*, Maria *mia*, when we have *each other*? We still carry our traditions with us—inside our hearts where they can keep us strong."

Signore Fanzini got so choked up when he realized his family was safe at last, he nearly began to cry. Wiping a tear from his eye, he cleared his throat. "Don't you women fall apart on me; you have a show to do. In just a few minutes the big top will be filled with people waiting for the Fanzinis to perform."

"That's right," Gino said. "But what about the magic act, Grandpa? There's a big hole in the show now that Loogastric is gone."

Armando began to roar with laughter. "Then we shall fill it with Fanzinis. And we shall make our own magic, just as we have for two hundred years!"

And so they did. That night's performance was indeed magical. The Fanzinis leapt higher, galloped faster, and performed more bravely than they ever had before. Their hearts lightened, their worries gone, they poured all their gratitude into their work. The crowd roared back its admiration and respect.

Each performer created a work of art—each act a masterpiece that would disappear after the performance, to be created anew the next night.

And so it was—the next night and the next, for the Fanzinis held the secret of *true* magical power. For two hours each night they could captivate an audience and make them forget all worldly cares.

They held within their company the timeless power of the circus: to delight through skill and spectacle. They had the ageless gift which had been passed on through thousands of years of tradition.

Chapter Fourteen

THE JOY OF A CIRCUS ARRIVAL IS EQUALED IN INTENSITY OF feeling only by the sadness of its departure.

The morning the Fanzinis were scheduled to depart Monroe, Amy felt bad.

Jamie didn't. He had learned enough from his experiences to write a great project paper about the circus. He couldn't wait for school to start Monday so he could lord it over Nelson Rappaport.

Amy had not written anything.

As the early morning sun rose above the elm trees in the distance, Amy sat on the porch watching the rays glistening on the dewy leaves.

"C'mon," said Jamie, "let's run over to the circus grounds and watch them pack up."

"All right," she said without enthusiasm. Although she hated good-byes, Amy wanted to bid farewell to the troupe in person.

119

As the twins neared the football field they could see traces of the early morning mist on the huge canvas of the big top. The old sailmaker was already at work, making his daily repairs with needle, cord, and patches. But inside the tent everything had been removed: seats, carpeting, and lights were all gone. Now it truly looked like a ship, minus people, crew, and cargo; and the huge canvas itself looked like a sail in the mist, about to push off for parts unknown.

Amy glanced around, her heart saddened by a sense of finality. The cheers, laughter, and applause were now things of the past, only echoes in her mind. She had wanted the circus to remain forever, but now it was leaving.

Gino ran into the tent and waved toward the twins. "Hi, I saw you guys coming."

"We wanted to say good-bye," Jamie said.

"So did I. I needed to thank you again for all you did for us."

"It wasn't anything," Jamie said, "just simple logical deduction."

"No, it was more than that," Gino said. He looked straight at Amy. "When you saved my life the other night, that got me thinking. It made me realize something fishy was going on, and that's when me and Rick began to investigate." He handed Amy the box he held in his hands. "So I want you to have this," he explained, "to remember me by."

Amy opened the box. Inside was Gino's white cape, which he had worn during the circus parade. "It's my very best one," he said.

"It's beautiful," Amy said. "Thank you."

"Maybe when you look at it, you'll think of me sometimes, okay?" Gino dug his sneakers into the dirt, blushed slightly, then looked away. "Well, I've got to go now. I promised to help with the packing up."

"How far are you going?" Amy asked.

"Eighty miles. We're performing in Sweetbriar tomorrow night."

"You're lucky," Jamie said, "you get to travel all over the country."

"I guess," Gino said wistfully. "Only sometimes—well, sometimes it's hard saying good-bye, you know?"

Amy knew. Emotion welled up inside her as she watched Gino hurry away.

It was now time to unlace the canvas of the big top. Crewmen hurried to all sides of the tent, loosening the quarter poles and the cable that held up the bail ring. Within moments the big tent fell to the ground with a giant *whoosh*.

Then Rick walked Betsy, one of his elephants, around the stake lines. Betsy was wearing a harness with a chain attached. Rick snatched the chain a few turns around each stake, then as he gave Betsy a signal she lifted the heavy metal stake from the ground as easily as if it were a straw. After that the canvas was carefully folded and placed on a flat truck.

Jamie marveled at the speed and efficiency with which the workmen proceeded.

Signore Fanzini and his wife walked by, supervising all the last-minute details. "Ah, our two little friends," said Armando, smiling. "You have come to see us off?"

121

"That's right," Jamie said, "we wanted to say good-bye."

"No, never say that," Lorenza Fanzini chided. "The circus never says farewell. Each spring we return again."

Her husband agreed. "Yes, when the little flowers in the field pop up, the Fanzinis will be back again—bigger and better than ever."

"Nothing could be better than your show last night," Jamie said. "Everyone was terrific."

"When our hearts are light, our bodies can sing," said Armando.

"So now you're a poet, Papa?" his wife said teasingly.

"And why not?" he replied joyously. "Our troubles are over!"

The Fanzini Troupe's big troubles might have been over, but the everyday problems of assembling and disassembling the circus still continued. The animals had to be fed before their long ride on the trucks and trailers.

As the twins said their farewells to Armando and Lorenza, Rick came running toward them. "Signore, someone must've stolen the treats I set aside for my elephants."

"What treats?" asked Jamie.

"I always give my bulls a special treat on moving day," Rick explained. "I had a nice bucket of fresh herbs set aside to put into their lunch. Now it's gone."

"Who would steal such a thing?" asked Signore Fanzini.

Amy stared at her brother. She remembered the special "menu" Cagliostro needed to rejuvenate himself: May dew and fresh herbs.

Jamie shrugged but did not say anything. At the age of twelve, Jamie had already shaped the man that he would someday be: always skeptical, idolizing reason and logic, and wary of all that did not fit neatly within that framework. In the sunny light of a spring morning he had drawn his final conclusions regarding the events of the past few days. Loogastric had no magic powers beyond that of illusion and hypnotism—the hallmarks of any circus magician. He was clearly a con man who had duped his companion into doing all the dirty work. As for the diamond necklace, its whereabouts would remain a mystery as it always had in the past.

Amy felt differently. She knew that somewhere not far away in the countryside, Cagliostro had found his one faithful companion and was now insuring his immortality.

It was nearly midday when the Fanzini Troupe finally departed from Monroe. Amy and Jamie stood on the barren football field, watching the trucks and trailers slowly weave down the road on their way toward Sweetbriar. The circus assembly looked like a huge, sluggish caterpillar bobbing up and down along the bumpy road.

As she waved good-bye Amy hoped they would all return again the following spring—and all the springs thereafter. She especially hoped Gino would be with them. Perhaps when she was all grown up, she would take her children to the circus, eager to catch a glimpse of the trapeze artist she had once known when they were both very young.

She hoped so.

EVERY CHILD DESERVES A GREAT BEGINNING!

Start with

DELL YOUNG YEARLING BOOKS!

Polka Dot Private Eye #1:
THE MYSTERY OF THE BLUE RING
  by Patricia Reilly Giff

Polka Dot Private Eye #2:
THE RIDDLE OF THE RED PURSE
  by Patricia Reilly Giff

Polka Dot Private Eye #3:
THE SECRET AT THE POLK STREET SCHOOL
  by Patricia Reilly Giff

Share-A-Story:
THE TREASURE SOCK
  by Pat Thomson and Tony Ross

STARRING FIRST GRADE
  by Miriam Cohen

BLACKBERRIES IN THE DARK
  by Mavis Jukes

LIAR, LIAR, PANTS ON FIRE!
  by Miriam Cohen

For a complete listing of these titles, plus many more, write to us at the
address below and we will send you the Dell Readers Service Listing.

DELL READERS SERVICE LISTING
P.O. Box 1045
South Holland, Illinois 60473

Twins Amy and Jamie are up to their ears in mysteries... and ghosts!

MOSTLY GHOSTS

by Mary Anderson

☐ **#1 THE HAUNTING OF HILLCREST**
$2.50   43372-X

☐ **#2 THE LEIPZIG VAMPIRE**
$2.50   44719-4

☐ **#3 TERROR UNDER THE TENT**
$2.50   48633-5

Dell

At your local bookstore or use this handy coupon for ordering:

DELL READERS SERVICE, DEPT. DMA
P.O. Box 5057, Des Plaines, IL. 60017-5057

Please send me the above title(s). I am enclosing $_____. (Please add $1.50 per order to cover shipping and handling.) Send check or money order—no cash or C.O.D.s please.

Ms./Mrs./Mr. _____

Address _____

City/State _____ Zip _____

DMA-2/88

Prices and availability subject to change without notice. Please allow four to six weeks for delivery. This offer expires 8/88.

SHOP AT HOME FOR QUALITY CHILDREN'S BOOKS AND SAVE MONEY, TOO.

Now you can have Dell's Readers Service Listing filled with hundreds of titles including many fine children's books. Plus, take advantage of our unique and exciting bonus book offer which gives you the opportunity to purchase a Dell book for only 50¢.
Here's how!

Just order any five books at the regular price. Then choose any other single book listed (up to a $5.95 value) for just 50¢. Write to us at the address below and we will send you the Dell Readers Service Listing.

DELL READERS SERVICE LISTING
P.O. Box 1045
South Holland, IL 60473